S0-ARY-478

CIRCLE VIEW

Circle View

stories by

Brad Barkley

Southern Methodist University Press
Dallas

These stories are works of fiction. Names, characters, places, and incidents are either the product of the author's imagination or are used fictitiously.

First edition, 1996

Requests for permission to reproduce material from this work should be sent to:
Rights and Permissions
Southern Methodist University Press
PO Box 750415
Dallas, TX 75275-0415

The stories in this collection first appeared in the following publications: "Under Water" in the *Greensboro Review;* "Circle View" in the *Florida Review;* "EAT" in the *Oxford American;* "Porter's Dodge" in *Cimarron Review* and *Republish;* "Knots" in *Tampa Review;* "The Extent of Fatherhood" and "The Singing Trees of Byleah, Georgia" in the *Georgia Review;* "Clown Alley" in *Willow Springs;* "The New Us" in *Southwest Review;* "Yagi-Uda" in *Chattahoochee Review;* "Spontaneous Combustion" in *Other Voices;* "Smoke" in *Glimmer Train;* and "Escaping" in the *Virginia Quarterly Review.*

Grateful acknowledgment is made for permission to quote lyrics from "Dream a Little Dream of Me." Words by Gus Kahn, Music by Wilbur Schwandt and Fabian Andree. TRO © Copyright 1930 (Renewed) 1931 (Renewed) Essex Music, Inc., Words and Music, Inc., New York, Don Swan Publications, Miami Florida and Gilbert Keyes Music, Hollywood, CA. Used by Permission.

Library of Congress Cataloging-in-Publication Data
Circle view : stories / by Brad Barkley. — 1st ed.
p. cm.
ISBN 0-87074-410-0. — ISBN 0-87074-411-9 (pbk.)
I. Title.
PS3552.A67137C57 1996
813'.54—dc20 96-33238

Cover art and design by Barbara Whitehead

Printed in the United States of America on acid-free paper
2 4 6 8 10 9 7 5 3 1

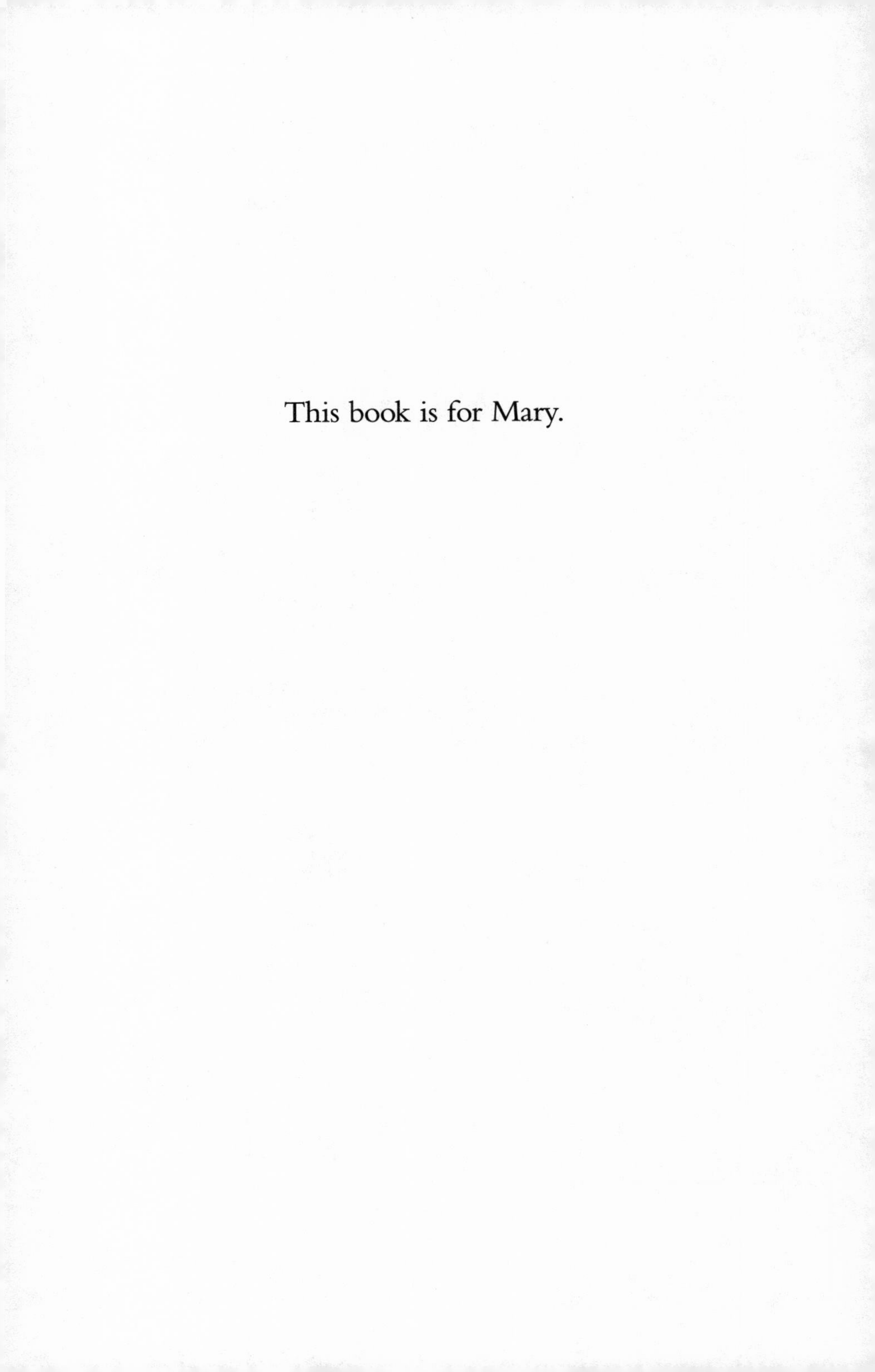

This book is for Mary.

Acknowledgments

Special thanks to my mother and father, to Lucas and Alex, and to Susan Perabo. Thanks also to Randolph Thomas, Steve Yates, John Thompson, Sidney Thompson, David Pratt, Jay Prefontaine, and the rest of the Saturday group. Also Skip Hays, Jim Whitehead, Joanne Meschery, Heather Ross Miller, Bill Harrison, Michael Heffernan, Brian Wilkie, Fred Chappell, Jim Clark, Lee Zacharias, and to Marie France and everyone in the Monday night Maryland group. Finally, I would like to thank the Maryland State Arts Council and the National Endowment for the Arts for their financial support.

Contents

UNDER WATER

I WORK my shift in the tunnel, so the Public Works boys stuck me with a nickname: "Mole." If they'd asked, I might have picked "Captain Nemo"—working beneath the tidewater, switching the dials, breathing by a gas mask in this drive-through submarine. My job is to keep traffic moving, flash speed limits and warning signs. Long, sodium-vapor days are spent manning the control board, hearing my own breath, and watching the numbers flash: average MPH, leak warnings, and what Ole Butt calls God's own LED, the CO level. On a given weekend, 143,000 passenger vehicles loop through Ocean Tides Tunnel, tourists bent on surf, sand, and knee-walking drunks. I swim in their fumes, live by the mercy of the mask.

The first commandment from Mole: *Stay In Your Lane.* Convertibles run zigzag, radios louder than all hell—wreck bait, headaches for yours truly. Sedans heed the signs our PW boys erect; two-wheelers won't make up their minds. Station wagons? Thank you, Lord, for station wagons. Above and beyond the call of traffic safety. Usually old people or young mothers, close enough to the tapered ends of life to have a feel for how eggshell fragile it is.

I learned that again myself, this past Sunday, at home with Marie and Gina. Marie turned her head and set aside her crossword, then drew my attention to the nursery-room wall, to a hepped-up whirring that hovered behind the sheetrock. A Waring blender on puree, I heard. A kazoo the size of a saxophone. With the corkscrew of my Swiss Army knife I managed a hole in the wall, and the wasps poured out like spent shells from an automatic, lofting to the ceiling full of pissed-off whining, bouncing off walls, off Gina's Snoopy mobile and tea set. Gina slept in her crib as the wasps, big and dark as peach seeds, found the soles of her tiny feet.

I snatched Gina off the mattress, flicking away wasps like cigarette butts and ignoring a sting I caught on my forearm. Marie jumped out the door shaking insects from her hair. I ran after and slammed the door behind me with the wasps ticking against it, a hailstorm in the spare bedroom. Marie shivered and Gina cried while I held them both, thinking what one wasp sting might do to a thirteen-month-old girl. I chewed cigarette tobacco and pressed it to Marie's wounds, then taped over the keyhole so none of the flying hell-bugs could escape.

"Warren, they could have *killed* her," Marie said. She leaned her ear against the nursery door, still shivering.

"But they didn't," I told her, stroking her hair. "We're safe."

Most that work the tunnel quit from claustrophobia. But Mole has too much of the real world (wasp attacks, cotton versus disposable) to let head-grown ideas take root. The walls of the tunnel sweat the brackish seawater and no sunlight finds me, but halogens carry their own light and the mask lets me breathe. So where, friends, is the claustrophobia when a man can see, hear, smell (the rubber of the mask), touch, taste (half-hour in the O booth for tuna on rye), and feel the big outdoors of family love in his chest? That night, Gina slept between us, her own bedroom still held hostage by mud daubers. Like an Allied spy in a war movie, I crept on hands and knees to the nursery door, snatched it open, and pitched a spewing insecticide bomb inside, then shoved the door closed. Two wasps escaped; one ended shoe-smacked against the smoke alarm, the other left its sting beside the perfect freckle below Marie's green eye (her other eye being blue). She screamed and cursed, grabbed the wasp and tossed like a crapshooter, dashing it against the wall.

By evening Marie looked the victim of a schoolyard bully and had shot a tube of Maybelline Cover-All to no avail (I told her she looked, as ever, beautiful). Gina needed clothes till we could get at her old ones, in the nursery-room dresser, so that night we made for Crabtree Mall. As we pushed the stroller, a short woman with choppy hair stepped up to us, looked at Marie's swollen and blackened eye, then stood on tiptoe, forehead to my chin.

"You bastard," she said to me. "You pig." She walked away, leaving me guilty as charged for allowing the wasp to escape. Then I understood—my own fists and temper had been accused of this crime. I laughed and shook my head, then saw the tears spill over Marie's swollen cheek like dew on an apple.

"Listen," she said at home. The bug bomb hadn't quieted the nursery-door hum. I thought of a thousand wasps wearing their own tiny gas masks.

"I hate this," she said. "It scares me, Warren. We aren't safe in our own home." And I understood. After the wasp attack, I spent the entire workday leaning over the catwalk rail, peering into passing cars to check that parents had their children safely buckled in car seats. When I saw a fat-kneed baby balanced on someone's lap, I jumped down and ran after, surprised to find myself thinking not one thing of babies and car seats, but of those wasps on Gina's feet. That night, Marie sent me to the hardware store to buy deadbolt locks for our doors and windows. I offered the obvious, that locks would not keep wasps out. "Wasps are a symptom," she said.

At the suggestion of Arco Exterminating, we vacated two days while they stormed the place like a SWAT team, a joke I found funny enough to repeat to the men who arrived on our porch with their yellow jumpsuits and pump jugs. We checked into Journey's End Econo-Stay, which featured a Wednesday night all-you-can-eat catfish buffet and Swirl-a-Jet bathtubs. The men from Arco found our entire house infested, I was told over the phone. We were lucky to be alive, the man said, those were no mud daubers but hornets; a swarm half the size of the one in our rafters could down a Jersey cow in five minutes. I didn't volunteer this for Marie, given her recent state. Besides, she seemed to enjoy the Journey's End, walking Gina down the hallways past the maid carts, throwing leftover biscuits to the gulls using the pool for the off-season, and taking long soaks in the Swirl-a-Jet. Though my days were spent in the tunnel, the rest of the time reminded me of my honeymoon: undertable hand-holding, fifty-one channels of cable, the magic of wrapped soap and maid service. One night, the three of us wore bathing suits and took turns splashing in and out of the churning bathwater. Marie, my mermaid, I said to her. Gina, my tadpole.

We returned to punchholes in the ceiling and sheetrock, the smell of insecticide, and the carcasses of what looked to be a million hornets littering our floor—our loveseat, shoetrees, and kitchen table—like spent firecrackers after a Chinatown parade. The workmen had left black thumbprints on the closet doors, half-empty styrofoam cups of coffee on the table. One hornet still buzzed against the windowpane in the looping throes of death, a terminal survivor of this bug battleground. Marie held Gina off the floor and minded her tiny grabbing hands, the dead insects crunching beneath Marie's sandals, blowing away at the breeze of her skirt. Two minutes of this erased two days of semi-honeymoon at the Journey's End. As Marie swept, her long hair spilled across her face, nearly hiding from my view her eyes and their thread of new tears.

For a week after, my arms sprouted gifts, flowers. I cooked that weekend, big shish kebabs for Marie and myself, and Gina's favorite, stewed carrots. Dessert wine followed, and "Yellow Rose of Texas" on my beat-up six-string. Marie sighed, rubbed my cheek with her palm. "You're trying too hard," she said.

"Follow the bouncing ball," I said to lead the sing-along, head wagging like a spring-neck dog in the back window of a Chevy. "Sing along with Mole."

"Don't call yourself that," Marie said, and my six rusty strings hummed to silence as she closed herself in behind the bedroom door.

The next night I arrived home from work and found Marie in the nursery, wiping ink from Gina's fingers, each stubby one tipped black.

"What's all this?" I asked.

"I'm fingerprinting her," Marie answered, not looking at me. On the dresser, a half-dozen Polaroids of Gina leaned against the Holly Hobby lamp, pictures in flat light, from the front and in profile, like most-wanted shots on the post office wall. A YWCA pamphlet lay on the bed, "Danger-Proofing Your Child."

"What are you charging her with?" I asked, trying for a joke.

"I'm protecting her," she said. "Making sure no one takes her."

"No one will take her. She's ours."

"You don't read the paper, Warren. You don't watch the news. You spend all day buried in that tunnel, no idea of what goes on."

She took new Polaroids once a week and bought an elastic leash to connect her wrist to Gina's for our trips to the mall or the park. She'd sit, biting her thumb, watching special news shows on inner-city drug gangs, and docudramas where they reenacted real-life crimes. One evening, when I'd had enough of sirens and sheeted bodies, I stood and snapped off the TV. Neither of us spoke to fill the quiet. Some nights I would wake at two or three to an empty bed and find Marie in the nursery, not feeding or changing Gina, but just looking at her from the doorway.

* * *

Saturday, the first day of spring, was the annual Public Works/Traffic Safety Iwo Jima Day at the Route 450 Survival Games Park. I boot-clomped downstairs for pancakes, decked out in camo, green face paint, goggles, and oak twigs pinned in my hair. Gina pointed, laughed, and said "Twee." That's right, Daddy's a tree, I told her, and scooped her into my arms. Tree frog, I called her.

"You're scaring her," Marie said, chenille bathrobe belted tight around her. My plate of cakes slid across the table.

"No, I'm not," I said, and raised in my defense my armload of giggling baby.

"No, you're not," Marie agreed. "I just wish you wouldn't go."

"I go every year."

"You don't have to go this year, Warren. It's dangerous. You fire bullets at each other."

"Paint balls," I said. "Harmless as rain." She shook her head. In past years Marie would kiss and salute me as I walked out the door, have chicken in the Weber and Bud on ice when I got home. The first year we'd dated she'd come with me, joined our squad, and shot Jim Munsun square in the butt.

Traffic Safety nabbed the PW flag in two hours. I got killed three times, one a clean headshot that left my hair stiff with paint, like old brushes in the basement. At home Marie was hanging laundry, skinny legs sticking out under a sheet. I pictured her sweet face, hidden, mouth full of clothespins. Still feeling combat-ready, I coasted to the end of the drive and slipped out the door, lifted Gina off the ground where she sat by the empty clothesbasket, tossing grass blades into it. I crept up, hoisted her, held her close to me. Tree frog, I whispered, then lifted her away from me and saw the red paint I'd forgotten about smeared across her head, and right then Marie stepped from behind the sheet, saw the bloodied two of us, and screamed so the pins fell from her mouth and disappeared in the grass. Before she calmed, before her hand could hold a cup steady, I had to box my camo and CO_2 gun, set them on the curb for Monday trash.

Marie's depression kicked her into reminiscence on the same day a 240 Volvo climbed the tunnel wall. Rain fell on Ocean Tides, cars entered the tunnel with wipers slapping. Pavement at both ends of the tunnel darkened with water pulled in by tires, the tires hissing as they ran through it. On the out-east side, the Volvo hit the darker stretch of asphalt as the blowout rebounded off the tunnel walls and reached my ears; it is a sound I know and am afraid of, not gunshot-loud but muffled, like a fat man punched in the stomach. I heard the fat-man punch, the rabbit squeal that followed, then felt the shake of ground beneath me as the crunch sounded, and I worried there might be children in the car. When I lifted my mask, the smell of gasoline was immediate, which meant foam trucks from OTFD.

After I'd radioed in, Joe Kreeger from the tollbooths ran down to describe the accident for me, the Volvo end-up against the tunnel wall, driver with a broken leg. By then, traffic had backed up past the in-east side, and drivers stood outside their cars, on the bumpers, trying to see the trouble. In-west traffic slowed from rubbernecking. I flashed a MAINTAIN POSTED SPEED for the west side, a FOR SAFETY'S SAKE, REMAIN IN YOUR VEHICLE for the east side. The CO level clicked off like a digital stopwatch, the motionless traffic making no breeze to wipe away its own poison. Colorless, odorless. Words I had memorized during training, till CO meant death to me in the simple way that for children death is a bad man, a bogeyman, for Marie is hornets and the evening news. I remembered Ole Butt, my supervisor, who on the day he gave us the masks held a number two pencil between thumb and forefinger.

"A hole this big," he said, "and you're breathing your own grave."

Those words bobbed to the surface of my brain as I watched the red LED blur, and I felt then the tonnage of seawater above and around me, felt myself enclosed in the poison air, buried like Jonah from Gina's *Golden Treasury of Bible Stories*—in the belly, praying for deliverance. Colorless. Odorless. But you can't bolt the door against gas any easier than hornets, and what else for Jonah to do—in the ocean, shadow of the whale behind him—but swim and swim and not look back? I set to work, trusting the mask and the men who made it.

At home Marie had Broadwater High School yearbooks spread across the rug, running her fingers over photos of boys in puka shells and earth shoes, girls in bandannas and mood rings, reading the faded autographs.

"Cleaning the attic?" I asked.

"Our parents never had to have us fingerprinted," she said. "Milk cartons had pictures of Elsie the Cow."

"So now we have ways to locate runaways. Progress."

"There. *Right* there," she said, standing, pointing at my chest. "Exactly the point. There *were* no missing kids then. Everyone stayed home. Things were safe."

"My uncle got killed on a bow-hunting trip in 1965."

"Accident," she said. "No one slit his throat in his bed. Sharon Beeler and I used to camp outside on the front lawn overnight. One year we hitchhiked to Myrtle Beach. Our front door stayed unlocked. No deadbolts."

"Everybody says things used to be better but it's not true," I said. "I helped my father dig a bomb shelter in our backyard, stocked it with gallon water jugs and C rations. He kept a rack of loaded twelve-gauges in the front hallway."

"You're remembering wrong, Warren," she said. "Deliberately remembering wrong."

Marie didn't speak much the rest of the evening, and I kept remembering wrong. The Wilsons, friends of my parents, whose boy suffocated in an abandoned refrigerator. The night at the drive-in when my father took away a jackknife from a teenage boy, snapped off the blade, and handed it back to him. Marie was watching a TV special, "Murder in Our Nation's Capital," and I picked up the senior yearbook to thumb through and find my own squirrelly picture. Someone had blackened out my front teeth. I found the picture of Coach Westafer, who cut me from roundball the first day out. "No such thing as a damned five-foot basketball player," he said. He wore a red T-shirt and a silver whistle. I can still hear him. I made all the games selling concessions, popping corn, and scraping sno-cones. After the last game of the season I walked up to Coach Westafer. "Five-foot-*four,"* I told him.

I got up from my chair and turned off the TV.

"Listen," I said to Marie, "let's us three go to a basketball game." I grinned watching the notion settle over her face. *"Gooo* Panthers," I said.

So we paid our six bucks (children under five free) and, with Gina on her elastic leash, stepped into the humid gym hung with championship banners and the American flag, alive with pinkish arc lamps and cheerleaders tossing a rustle of pom-poms. The game had just started, Panthers led by four. We found a spot in the bleachers to watch the gangly and muscled boys backpedal up the court, block above the rim, drive headlong for out-of-bounds balls, take two dribbles on foul shots. We sat with other adults, parents of the on-court teens. They went gooey over Gina, not having witnessed babyness in their own kids for a good fifteen years.

We stomped the bleachers, keeping time with the cheerleaders, who still wore dark blue short shorts under light blue skirts, snarling panthers chasing across their sweaters. Caught up, Marie stood to cheer, shouted at the referee, hugged a middle-aged woman beside her when we scored. I headed for the concession to see who held my old job. "Easy on the juice, kid," I said to the chubby boy scraping my sno-cone. I felt like an old sea captain addressing his first mate. "Don't want a soggy cup." Tough but fair. The Panthers' coach was not Coach Westafer, and when I asked I was told he'd moved to Charlotte four years ago, died of a stroke while stringing tomatoes in his garden.

After the Panthers won, we went for ice cream, Gina asleep on my shoulder. Marie's smile wouldn't leave her face, like a window shade that won't close.

"Man, overtime and we pulled it out. You see that one kid, number eleven? Six-eight, I bet, at least. And no more saddle shoes, did you notice?"

"So," I said, "did you have fun?"

She leaned across to kiss me. "The most," she said.

The excitement of the Panthers' ball game began to draw Marie away from her news shows and headlines, but gave me worry in a new way. Her evenings were spent in 1974, thumbing the yellowed pages of *Pine Burr,* the Broadwater yearbook. While I read the paper, Marie would interrupt with high-school trivia.

"Ethan Nash . . . whatever happened to him?"

"Don't even remember him," I said.

"Oh, you do, Warren. Always wore a leisure suit, never smiled."

Most evenings she'd end up on the phone with an operator in Texas or Illinois, tracking people she'd not seen in fifteen years. She began making plans to organize a reunion, and forgot Gina's Polaroid for that week and the next.

"Would you do something you didn't want to, if it was something I wanted?" Marie sprang this one on me one night at dinner. She served up the question with a sly grin, the first I'd seen in weeks. I laid down my fork.

"Sure I would," I answered, unsure where this was headed.

"I want to go to the Broadwater prom." She blushed, eyes on her plate. I looked at her.

"We're a bit long in the tooth for that, don't you think?" I winked at Gina in her high chair.

Marie hadn't gone to the prom as a student. (I knew her then, but only her name and the fact that she ran hurdles for the track team.) A nervous, too-tall girl, she'd contented herself with serving on the decorating committee, streaming the gym with crepe paper and Japanese lanterns with refrigerator bulbs inside. She pulled me to the bedroom to show me the teal bridesmaid dress she'd bought for Sandy Jenkins's wedding, and my own wedding tux, both newly back from the dry cleaners. She didn't lack for planning.

"They won't sell you tickets," I said, finding an easy out. "You're not a student."

"Don't you worry," she said, "I'll get the tickets."

And she did. I dropped her at the door the next afternoon, after school let out, and sat in the truck listening to traffic reports. Twenty minutes later she reappeared, fanning the tickets and grinning.

My Carolina Blue tux not only still fit but seemed big in the shoulders, like I'd shrunk. Marie emerged from the bedroom as if from a cocoon, gorgeous in the green dress (to match her left eye), her hair pulled up in a silky twist. I was struck beyond words.

After we'd dropped Gina at Mrs. Gutherson's, Marie told me the prom was not to be held in the gym but at Deer Run Country Club, tucked back in the rolling golf-course hills of the rich section. My battered Ford long-bed looked like some bastard son there in the curved driveway of the club, chugging and bouncing behind white stretch limos, an antique Rolls, and a flock of cars of a type I recognized from the tunnel: Daddy's Mercedes.

Inside pulsed a furious attack of colored lights and beat-heavy music that rattled my heart in its cage. Girls (blondes every one of them, it seemed) danced in ruffled and sequined Hollywood-premiere-type dresses Marie later guessed cost more than she'd spent to buy her wedding gown, the one that hung plastic-covered in the back of the closet to be handed down to Gina. I had to stop Marie from retrieving her coat and slipping it on over her dress. No 45s of Cat Stevens or Seals and Crofts played over the school PA, but instead a disc jockey danced on a platform in pink tie and top hat, shouting dirty jokes between the mortar blasts of drum-thumping music. Boys wore tails and hair mousse, carried ebony walking sticks, sported diamond studs in their earlobes. I stood there in my Carolina Blue tux with the dark blue piping and clip-on butterfly bow tie, trying to shout into the ear of my wife, who in her simple green dress still looked more beautiful than all the Zsa Zsas shaking themselves on the dance floor. What I might have told her, what I felt, is that you never really feel old till you bang your head up against youth.

We walked out past the chauffeurs sitting smoking on the hoods of their cars—men in black uniforms, most old enough to be fathers to the kids inside. We climbed in the truck and I spun out of there.

Marie sank down in her seat, slipped off her heels, and put her bare feet on the dash.

"I'm just dumb. And embarrassed," she said. "Why did I think that would be anything like what I missed?"

"What's that Stones' song? 'Time Waits For No One?' " I said. "I think they wrote that for us." She half-smiled.

"I made a fool of myself," she said, looking out the window. I took my hand off the gearshift and laid it over hers. "You look beautiful," I told her, and it was true. Her feet pressing the dash, green dress hiked up her thighs, wind at the top of her window trailing wisps of her done-up hair. She squeezed my hand, gave me a sad smile. We drove around, listening to the radio.

"Listen," I told her, "let's fetch the youngster."

"Yes. We're old, it's past our bedtime."

We picked up Gina, a sleepy bundle, from Mrs. Gutherson, and wrapped her in the car seat. At McNair I passed our turn and headed out onto the highway.

"Where are you going?" Marie asked. By now Gina was awake, making cooing sounds, trying out words.

"I want to show you where I work," I said. We were dressed up and the truck cab glowed faint green from the dash lights, night blew in the window warm and newly humid. A perfect spring evening, I didn't want to end it by going home.

"I've seen where you work a million times," she said. "We drive through every summer."

"You've never seen it like this," I answered. It was near eleven, traffic was sparse. Marie stared at me.

"You've never seen it on foot," I said.

"On foot! Warren, I am *not* walking inside that tunnel. We'll get hit by a car."

"We'll stay on the catwalk, three feet above the road."

I parked at the tolls and waved to Sheila and Junior, who worked the only two booths open at night. We walked down the in-west side, against the slope, the familiar tightening spreading along the front of my thighs. Marie carried her heels and we held Gina's hands between us. My steps reverberated off the walls as we descended to the level-off. Gina's slate-colored eyes opened wide, taking in the pink bead of sodium lights that ringed the curved ceiling above us. I kept reaching for a gas mask that wasn't there. With no traffic or heat, night wind pushed through the tunnel, moving the loose wisps of Marie's auburn hair. The cement walls sweated with damp, giving off a brackish, greenhouse smell. The sound of the wind was a faint whoosh.

"Listen," I whispered. Marie lifted Gina and the two of them were still.

"Wind?" Marie asked.

"Water," I said. "Ocean. We're in it, under it." Marie shrank back, eyeing the ceiling above us.

"We're safe," I told her, and rapped my knuckles on a concrete support beam.

Marie stepped across the catwalk, hugging Gina to her chest, dangling the high heels by their straps. She leaned and put her ear to the wall, as if the tunnel were a huge conch shell. The wind pushed, I closed my eyes. The faint sound *was* like that of the ocean—not crashing waves but deep currents, mid-ocean swells. I opened my eyes, leaned in toward my wife and daughter.

"The whole, big ocean out there," I said.

"Hear that, sweetie?" Marie said, jiggling Gina. "We're under the water, in the sea. Hold your breath," she told her, and made a show of drawing in air, puffing her cheeks. Gina laughed and copied her, and I did the same, the three of us making a game of it, holding our breath like swimmers and listening for the quiet ocean all around us.

Circle View

THROUGH gauzy curtains Red Burgess watched a man walk down the gravel road toward her house. His movements were slow, far off, waved by the heat, a mirage. Red bit her thumbnail and turned to look over her shoulder through the dust-coated hall out the back door. She saw her husband, King, on the asphalt lot, working the tangle of rusted wires that topped the speaker posts like stalks of dried-up corn. King Burgess, who had once made a game of calling her his queen—the Queen of the Circle View. Eleven years before, his easy words had lured her out of her senses and into a marriage.

The man had reached the down side of the road toward

the drive-in. A child or large dog loped beside him; from this distance Red could not tell which. Each year, two or three visitors found their door—men, usually, with broken down cars or bad directions, like paper scraps blown against a fence, drawn for miles off the flat horizon to the Circle View by the sagging brick projection tower. In winter, the tower dropped bricks on the roof of the house, loud thumps that on cold nights kept Red awake, staring at the ceiling, while in the next room King snored and muttered in his bed.

A small child—a girl—trotted to keep up with the man. He moved like a bent wheel, Red thought. Then she saw: the man's one leg worked inside baggy trousers, tightening and puckering the fabric, and the other leg was not there, had been amputated high up, near his groin, the way a dog has a leg missing. The trouser leg had been cut away, and the man propelled himself on a pair of aluminum elbow crutches.

"My name's John Shire." The wiry man stood on her front porch, flashing bright movie star teeth. The pale, skinny girl, eight or ten, leaned beside him in a hounds-tooth dress. Her hair hung in dirty tangles to her shoulders.

"Car broke down," he said. The calluses of Red's hand warmed on the brass knob. She watched him hook the crutch handles over his arm and stand balanced, unswayed.

"No one lives out here," she told him, leaning her foot on the door. John Shire ran his hand through his thin hair. His muscled arms were decorated with green tattoos beneath black hair, the designs of the tattoos uncertain and smeared, like ink pulled up by a blotter. His cutaway left trouser leg had been knotted up with twine.

"Lost and gone, ma'am," he said. "Headed for Texas and missed my turn."

A paper scrap, Red thought, like most of the visitors each year—the drifters, confused UPS drivers, broken downs from the highway into Tulsa. Parents sometimes dragged their bored children to the Circle View, to show them how things were in the old days. Those Red turned away—no movies had been run in fifteen years. She would point to the marquee out front, which displayed no titles, only rock holes, two broken letters, and an abandoned bird's nest. King reminisced with those same visitors over the magic days of drive-in movies, and extracted from them a promise to return the next year, when, bet-your-bottom-dollar, he told them, he would be back in business.

"We could do with a good pull of water," John Shire said.

A dust devil twirled like a child in the yard, circling toward the house. Red moved to allow the man inside. The girl followed, and Red closed the door.

"How you drive without two good legs?" she asked him. John Shire grinned.

"Still got two good legs," he said. Red glanced at his knotted-up trousers and felt her face warm.

"King will fix your car," she said, pointing her chin toward the dirty window, toward King in the back lot. John Shire moved, leaning into the metal crutches, his arm muscles working like small animals beneath the skin. The girl sat in King's worn leather chair and began playing with the fireplace poker. Out back of the brick house was the drive-in, or what remained of it. King was dressed like a golfer in madras pants, a yellow alligator shirt, and a Panama hat. He had looked the same the day Red met him, back in Shelby, when he'd come into her junk shop tracking down a commercial popcorn maker. She listened to him describe his plans for the Circle View, watched his fingers smooth across the mahogany top of a Victrola. Red could find no nostalgia, no longing or ache, in treadle sewing machines or washboards, only money for the light bill. What she couldn't sell she'd discard. But in this King Burgess, big and ruddy-faced among the Flexible Flyers, oak rockers, and Elvis whiskey decanters, she had heard a pining love for the past and, more importantly, a chance for good business. She had left with him the next week.

In the kitchen, Red blew the dust from two glasses and filled them with water, then topped off the jar of dark wine she had been drinking.

"I get it," John Shire said as he took the glass. "That's your daddy."

"My husband." She waved her wedding band, stuck on her finger.

They watched King work to reattach one of the window speakers to its pole, the rows of speaker poles like a stunted orchard grown out of broken asphalt, clumps of weeds, and scattered chips of paint peeled off the house. The glass-bead screen at the back of the property, punched through with holes, had one white corner bent over, like a worn page in a story book.

"I get it," John Shire said again. "A real mom-n-pop operation. You cook chili dogs, the old man runs movies, boys park their cars and bird-dog their best girlfriends."

"There's none of that out here," Red said. She glanced at the girl, who still had not spoken. The girl looked at Red and blinked, then groped between the cushions of King's chair, pulling out paper clips and linking them into a chain. John Shire grinned and stared openly at Red's chest, which made her look down at herself—the torn T-shirt and faded jeans, slippers held together with duct tape. She gathered her hennaed hair away from her shoulders to pull it back,

and immediately regretted raising her arms, which lifted her breasts. She looked away.

"The drive-in isn't working," she said. "Hasn't had any business for fifteen years, since before we owned it." King convinced her they'd fill the place every night with family classics shown on the four-story screen, concessions sold in the booth lit by yellow bug lights. She'd auctioned off the junk store (except what King insisted they keep) and moved here with him. Factory layoffs in the area had been like opening a drain, the town and businesses, all the people, funneling away. Then changes to the county roads put them on a dead-end and stirred up the dust that settled like a blanket over the decaying body of the Circle View. King worked day and night the first year—patching pavement, rewiring, pulling weeds. Evenings, he would spill on the kitchen floor cardboard boxes full of four-inch plastic letters, arrange them to spell out titles of movies as they would appear on his marquee. Like a kid playing with blocks, she thought. He spent five thousand of what they had saved on a new projector, then, fooling himself that they were close to opening, blew the rest ordering from catalogs prints of his favorite movies—*National Velvet, Citizen Kane, Swiss Family Robinson, Dr. Zhivago*—before they had a new screen to show them on, or car speakers to hear them. Red thought the movies were awful, the kind people watched on Sunday afternoons with a hangover and baseball rained out. They'd do better money, she told him, with dirty movies, the X-rateds. Red knew business, what people would pay to see. But King said he wouldn't have his lot full of men in smelly raincoats, and besides, he believed interest in sex was diminishing. Especially here at home, had been Red's silent answer to this. Silent, because King's worries over the difference in their ages and his inability to, as he put it, "satisfy her desires" had drawn her, those first years, into a habit of reassurance. King would hug her, pinning her arms and rubbing her back, her cheek pressed to the plastic buttons of his sweater, his pink skin dry and dark spotted.

"I still need you like this, your companionship," he would say to her. She had, for those years, kept her silence, then one night come to the end of it. King had hugged her, rubbed her back, told her what he still needed. She opened her dried lips against the wool and cold buttons of his sweater.

"And I need a good fuck," she said, biting the words.

She felt the rush of heat rise in his doughy neck as she backed away from him. He turned from her, and had not touched her since; she had not wanted him to. They occupied the house like furniture. His Navy pension paid the necessities and not much else. King settled into tinkering with the Circle View the way other men his age puttered in a vegetable garden. The only difference, Red often thought, is that those men don't rely on a garden for everything, won't starve if it goes bad.

Red introduced King to John Shire. King shook his hand and asked Shire if he'd come to be disabled while serving his country. John Shire saluted and answered "Yes sir," then cut his eyes at Red and winked. He looked nice when he did that, she thought. Like someone who could turn trouble into a good time. King bent down toward his leather chair, the heat of sunburn radiating off the back of his neck.

"And who might this be?" he asked the pale girl. She smiled, her lips pulled back like the skin of a cut.

"Rose," she said. "Rose Shire." They were the first words she had spoken.

"What brings you out to visit me?" King asked her.

"Daddy's car broke down," she said. "We're playing a joke on Mama." Red and King both looked at John Shire.

"Where she gets these ideas," he said.

They walked out to examine the broken-down Chevy Nova, Red drinking wine from her jar, King carrying his big wooden toolbox. John Shire made small grunts with the effort of working the crutches amid bits of broken concrete. Red walked behind him, watching the jump of muscle beneath the taut, brown skin of his arms, following the rhythm as he worked the crutches, his elongated triceps twitching like snakes. His smell was a mix of cologne and cigarettes.

Inside the yellow car was a homemade rigging of ropes, coat hanger wires, and levers made from two-by-twos, slick and dirty with wear. King deemed it all worthy of Rube Goldberg; John Shire said no, he'd thought it all up himself. It allowed him to drive with just his hands.

"Here, Ace," John Shire said to King. "Let me show you what works." The engine had quit on him, he explained, and would not start. King soon found the problem under the hood. A coat hanger wire leading from a small lever on the dash, through the firewall, to the choke had kinked and caught around the fuel line. In two minutes, it was fixed and running.

"What's the heart of an engine?" King asked, his head still under the hood. Flecks of grease dirtied the tail of his golf shirt.

"Not a clue," John Shire answered.

"Carburetor—yours is black, carbon fouled. Stay for dinner, I'll clean her up for you."

"Okay," John Shire said, his voice empty of gratitude. King scratched his head under his hat.

"Or stay the night, and in the morning I'll patch that

muffler for you, before you go deaf." He shouted over the engine noise to emphasize his point.

"Ain't got anywhere to be." John Shire looked at Red and smiled big. A swirl of dust kicked up and blew around them. She squinted against the flying grit, her eyes blurry with tears. The white of John Shire's movie star teeth shone like snow in the sun, nearly blinding her before she shut her eyes completely.

* * *

After King had the carburetor apart and soaking in kerosene, he went out back to finish his job on the speaker stalks. Rusted out connections had to be resoldered, and new wiring was needed leading to the main switch box in the projection tower on the back of the house. Rose followed him out and knelt on the tacky pavement beside him, her hands curled like dried leaves in her lap. King explained every step as he performed it, named for her the different tools in his box so she could hand them to him when he asked. She said nothing, would offer her smile, gums and small teeth, when he looked at her. He began asking for the tools with made-up names—Sammy Screwdriver, Wanda Wirecutters—trying to coax a laugh from her. One of the stray cats, the flop-eared one, appeared from around the house. The cat's ear was bent over, King told her, to mark its place in a fight. She grinned. To King it seemed somehow as if she wanted to laugh and simply didn't know how, the way he'd like to be able to play piano and couldn't.

"We get this all wired up, see," King said to her. "Patch up the screen and rebead it, crank the projector, fire the marquee, open the gates and boom!—we're in business."

"What's it for?" Rose asked.

"What's what for?"

"Screen," she said. "Rebead, marquee, protector."

"Projector," King said. "For showing movies, of course."
She looked at him.

"You know movies?" King asked. "You've seen them."
She shook her head.

"Then you've seen them on TV. Not the same, but better than nothing."

"Daddy busted out the TV," she said.

King could only look at her, her pale face reddening from the sun and heat of asphalt. How to describe movies for her? He might as well try to describe the ocean to a blind man.

"Movies are stories," he started.

"Tell me one." Her pinched face brightened. "Tell me a movie."

"Stay here," he said. She stood, her thin knees red and dimpled with bits of gravel. King walked to the garage and pulled his Olds 88 to the lot, steering around chunks of pavement and broken bottles. He slid into the space beside the newly wired speaker. Dusk was near, the sky a liquid blue, the parking lot giving back its saved heat to the cool evening. King motioned to Rose; she came around to the passenger side and climbed in, slamming the door. King rolled down the window to unhook the speaker from its post. He stretched the coiled wire and hung the metal box on the window ledge.

"Watch the screen," he told her, and she slid forward on the seat, hands against the dash. "Once upon a time," he said—and realized he hadn't thought of what to tell her, that he had never, in fact, told a story to a child. Rose cut her eyes at him. He could think only of his favorite movie, *Citizen Kane.*

"Once there was a rich man," he began.

"Like you," Rose said, and grinned.

"Well, okay." King smiled at her and pulled off his hat to keep it from hitting the headliner. His hair, he saw in the rearview, was the color of a honeydew melon. The hat had left a dent in his hair, circling his head.

"The man's name was Kane, and he was old, but when he'd been a boy his father wasn't nice to him, and beat him." Rose lowered her face and looked into her lap. "Watch the screen," King said quietly.

"Kane had a sled he loved very much, and when he grew up he got to be rich as a prince and sold newspapers. He had a wife and a son who died, then he married a singer." King faltered, realizing it might not be the right story for a child, trying to leave out parts about divorce and adultery, about Susan leaving Kane, Kane sliding into despair, dying alone. Instead, King played up Kane's glass ball with the snow scene inside, the fact that at the end of his life he still loved his sled, which—King made a big show of telling her—had been called Rosebud. He did not tell her the glass ball got broken, the sled burned.

"That's almost your name," he said. "Rosebud." At this she did laugh, the car too dark for him to see her.

"I wish I could tell it better," he said. At times he had tried to describe his favorite movies for Red, but she wasn't interested in hearing, or in movies at all, for that matter. Why pay three dollars for a movie, she always asked, when you could read a book for free? But she never read books, only watched soap operas on her little black and white TV, the screen no bigger than King's hand. She watched them all day now, a vinegar jar and rag in her lap to wash dust from the tiny screen. When King passed through the room she said nothing, or worse, spoke sentences that had nothing in them. This was the way it had been since he last touched her. *I need a good fuck.* Nights, her words came back to him, stealing his sleep. He would rise from bed in darkness, step quietly to the latrine and remove his pajamas to study himself in the mirror—the flabbiness he had aged into, his lifeless, flaccid penis. His body, still sturdy, had turned against him, been derelict in its duty. He would silently curse it, curse Red's unhappiness with him and his dislike for her, before he drew on his pajamas and got into bed, trying to find sleep before morning.

"I like that snowball," Rose said. In the dark her shining eyes still watched the giant screen, which glowed in the dusk like a sheet that had been forgotten on the line and left out overnight.

Inside, King watched Red unfold his old Navy cot and throw sheets over the couch for their guests. She warmed the food and called everyone in, blowing dust off the table before setting the places.

They sat to dinner, Shire leaning his arms on the table, hovering over his plate. The muscles in his face worked with chewing. He clutched his fork, shoveling in the food. Shire looked up and saw King looking at him.

"So, Pop," he said, "I see you pulled your car around. We having a show tonight? Open for business?"

"Well, no. Not exactly." King felt the sunburn on his face.

"C'mon, Pop, you can tell me. A little *Deep Throat,* huh? Choke your chicken? Red knows what I'm talking about." King watched John Shire smile and wink at Red. To his surprise, she blushed and grinned as she swallowed wine from her jar. He thought of the first days of their marriage, when she would come to him, naked and flushed.

"How's the car, boss?" Shire said. "Don't know what I'd do if I got stuck here." He smiled at King, knife and fork in his fists.

"Your car will be driveable first thing in the morning," King said, "if you'd care to leave."

"Whatever you say, boss."

"Do you have a snowball?" This came from Rose, her skinny arms, like her father's thick ones, propped on the table. The question seemed not to be directed toward anyone in particular.

"Snowballs in July. What a dumbshit." John Shire snorted a laugh. Red gave him a smack on the arm. King looked at her.

"A snowball, Mr. King," Rose said. "Like the man in the movie." King mentally sorted through the boxes they had saved from the junk shop; the closest thing to a snow dome he could remember seeing was a set of Currier and Ives plates.

"We'll have to see, sweetheart."

"I'll fetch dessert," John Shire said, and hopped to the cabinet beneath the sink, brought back the bottle of Wild Turkey. King could never remember where to find the bottle himself, and was startled by this man's familiarity with their kitchen. John Shire uncapped the bottle, poured into the cups that had been set out for coffee. As he raised his cup, Red raised hers and they clinked.

"Hi-de-ho," he said.

Red laughed, shook her head. "John, you're a stitch." Her face shone with high color, and her teeth, when she laughed, were wet and bright. "King, don't you think John's a stitch?"

John Shire lifted the bottle and refilled the cups, doubling the untouched portion in King's cup. He lowered the bottle, then, as a second thought, raised it to pour half an inch into Rose's empty milk glass.

"Drink it down before it swims away." Rose lifted the glass and licked her lips. King laid his hand across her wrist, not much thicker than the grip of his putter.

"Honey, no. Not for children."

John Shire gestured, sloshing drink across the chicken bones on his plate. "Hell, let her drink it. I started younger than her, never hurt me."

"Maybe she shouldn't," Red said. "But when I was little and had a cough, my mama used to give me a tiny shot of whiskey."

"Well, there you go," John Shire said. "She gets the hooch and doesn't even have to bother with a cough."

Rose lowered her face to the rim of the glass, sniffed, wrinkled her nose.

"Honey, please," King said. She looked at King and grinned, handed the glass over to him.

"Suture yourselves," John Shire said. "More for me."

* * *

After dinner, King and the girl headed for the concession booth out back, where King had promised to let her see the cotton candy machine. King left holding her skinny hand. The kid bothered Red, nothing but pale bones and that gash of a smile. It always surprised her how much King liked children, how they reacted toward him. She'd seen it before, on trips to the grocery store with him. Kids would search him out, as if in his bright clothes he were a clown sent to entertain them. Early in their marriage he had asked Red for children, spoken the words to her back as she lay curled to the side of the bed they once shared. Now, even if she did want children, he wouldn't be able. His problem, he called it. Her problem too.

"That kid's in for a disappointment," Red told King. "Nothing to spin in that machine but cobwebs and dust. If the damn thing worked."

"My dear, you forget the power of pretend," he said. No, she hadn't, she thought. Her own happiness had operated on it for eleven years.

After King and Rose left, Red poured a bourbon for herself and another for John Shire. The day had produced on him a shadow of beard, like a backdrop to those white teeth. When he scratched his neck, the coarse whiskers rasped, brown skin taut across his jutting Adam's apple. Red thought of King with his golf shirts buttoned to the neck, the roll of flesh pushed out, soft as wet sand. John Shire seemed solid and flat as an ironing board, his muscles connecting hard angles of bone and sinew, his movements as exact and purposeful as the rope and levers rigged in his car. Such easiness and grace she saw in how he tilted a glass, set his elbows on the table, smiled, that she forgot, sitting with him, that part of him was missing.

"How did you lose your leg?" she asked. He looked at her several moments without speaking; she began to think it was the wrong question, something he didn't talk about.

On his twenty-eighth birthday, he explained, he and some friends sat on the tracks in the woods near town, smoking dope and flinging beer bottles at trees. When the headlights of the sheriff's jeep found them, they scattered. John Shire took off across the trestle, where the jeep couldn't follow. He stepped quickly in the dark, smelling the creosote that made his boots tacky on the ties. A hundred feet below shone the creek, dark as oil in the moonlight, against which he saw the ties in silhouette, feeling his way with his feet to avoid the ten inches of open space in between. With too much to smoke he began to watch the moon reflected in the water, floating there like a ball dropped down, and twenty feet from the end of the trestle he stepped between and down through, his thigh wedged hard between the ties. Stuck. He stopped his story and grinned.

"So, what do you think happens next?"

"God," she said, and shut her eyes. A chill pricked her spine. "The train."

"Nothing. I waited for the damn train, got myself ready for it, even prayed for it once or twice, but nothing. Sun came up a couple times. I slept and passed out, shouted when I could think of it. After three days I'd lost enough weight or the leg had withered enough to wedge it back out. Dead when I pulled it out, gangrene. I hauled it back to town and it weighed heavy as a young'un." John Shire reached and with his hands shaped in the air his missing thigh.

"It hurts, what's missing. Hurts like a bitch."

Red's own legs had gone numb where she sat at the edge of her chair. She closed her eyes, trying to hear the sound of the creek, the groan of wooden beams beneath the trestle. But there was only the familiar silence, a dust-heavy quiet. Red opened her eyes and put her hands around John Shire's fingers, both of them now holding the missing limb.

"You ain't stuck," he whispered.

* * *

As he entered the projection tower and started up the wooden stairs, King held Rose's hand, tiny, fragile as bird bones. At the top was the projection booth, a room he'd not visited for a year. Insulation was gone from the lightbulb wire that dangled from the ceiling—chewed away, he imagined, by mice. Dust coated the room, the movie print boxes stacked on the floor, the plastic tarp thrown over the projector. Stacked in corners were crates of things they'd saved from Red's junk shop: washboards, odd pieces of depression glass, wind-up toys. Rose found the toys and set them off, let them clatter on the floor, stirring dust.

King emptied a box marked "Odds and Ends" in what he recognized as his own handwriting. Inside, near the bottom, he found what he'd searched for: a glass snow dome. When he lifted it he discovered it was not glass but plastic; inside, an elephant held in his trunk a banner that read "Goldwater in '64." Liquid in the dome had evaporated, and the snow scratched inside like grains of sand.

"Look what I found," King said. Rose looked up from the toys, reached to take the snow dome. She held and then shook it, frowned. This was not the magical item he'd described for her, was not at all like Charles Kane's talisman; it was, simply, a piece of junk. King shrugged and took it back from her, set it on the ledge of the glass projector window.

"Come look." He turned over a crate for her to stand on to see out, held her shoulders and pointed. He remembered he had shown Red this same view the first day he brought her out here with him.

"A beam of light comes out of the machine," he said to Rose. "Travels over the heads of the people in their cars, shines on the screen. People watch the light on the screen, the stories carried in it, and they laugh or feel sad." She stood without speaking, her gaze focused toward the square of white screen. Behind her, King saw her pale face reflected in the tiny window, could see the shine and flicker of her eyes searching the dark. Below, he heard the back screen door click shut, and cupped his hands to the window to see. He patted Rose on the shoulder.

"You go on to bed now, honey. You're tired."

She leaned and kissed his cheek before she stepped off the crate and headed downstairs toward the cot set up for her by the open front window. King snapped off the bulb, cupped his hand to the glass, and, as his eyes adjusted to the dark, saw the slow-moving figure of Red, the pale blue of her shirt—beside her, the drunken ease with which John Shire moved on his crutches. They stopped, and Red swung a bottle to her lips. It glinted in the moonlight like a blade and made him think of a sword swallower in a movie he'd once seen. Red held the bottle for John Shire to drink, then wiped his chin with her finger. King watched them pick their way across the lot and swing open the door of his Olds, still parked beside the speaker in the expanse of black pavement littered with bright shards of glass. They bent and climbed in the back seat, the oily glint of John Shire's hair visible beside flashes of her white skin. They moved in close to one another, then sank, past where he could see them, as if sinking in a pool.

"I won't allow it," he whispered, aware of Rose downstairs. He pressed his fingers to the glass, and watched for several minutes. They did not reappear. As King turned from the window, his elbow knocked the snow dome and he caught it before it fell. He thought again of *Citizen Kane,* of what he'd left out as he told the story to Rose. King tipped his hand to let the plastic snow dome fall to the floor, where it did not shatter but skitted across the floor in the dark, the dried bits of snow rattling inside.

* * *

She packed everything out of her chest of drawers (from a Maryland estate sale, she remembered), and half of what hung in the wardrobe. Her suitcase bulged, though they would be gone only the weekend. She remembered the Motel 6 on the highway. John Shire had seen it on the way in. In the back seat of the Olds she had leaned into his wide, leathery hands pressed to her spine, her right thigh spread across the upholstery where his own left leg should have been. He'd worked her body, the parts of her, much as she imagined him working the ropes and levers in his car, and she gave in to it, left herself to the memory of her skin, to her own near-forgotten ability to draw heat from a man. And as easily as he manipulated his car, John Shire brought her over familiar but neglected ground to a place where she knew she wanted to stay.

"One weekend," he'd told her. "Clean sheets, maid service. Queen-size bed, beer in the bathtub."

"You're forgetting your little girl. We can't just leave her."

"I ain't forgetting. Uncle King won't mind baby-sitting a couple nights."

She had not, for some reason, thought of King till then. But what would he do when she came back on Monday? Nothing, just as he would do nothing now to stop her leaving. Impotence was like cancer—unchecked, it spread. King oozed it, and on Monday she could walk in the kitchen and poach eggs, hand King his buttermilk and remind him to wear his hat. If she had to explain, she would tell him the weekend had been a break in the dull movie of their lives, like when the projectionist forgets to change the reel and for a moment the screen flares white. He could say nothing, though, knowing as she did that she should be gone, away from him and this place he'd brought her to, where she felt her life, like everything around them, given over to dust, awaiting slow burial.

She brought her bag downstairs and out the door, tossed

it in the back of John Shire's car. Then she sat on the hood of the Nova to wait, leaned her head on the windshield. Overhead, the moon shone at the phase she could never remember the name for, full but for a thin edge broken off, damaging the perfect circle.

* * *

Through his bedroom window King watched her, her rust hair spread across the windshield of the Nova. He had awakened hearing the dry whisper of clothes swept from the closet in the adjoining room—her bedroom—and pushed into a bag. Now she waited. King walked down to her, past Rose asleep on the cot in the front room.

"King, dammit, I'm going off for the weekend. I got to get away from here for a while."

"You aren't coming back," he told her, meaning, simply, that she wouldn't.

"Don't forget I own half this place, my name's on the deed." In the moonlight the colors of her clothes vanished, and she was rendered in black and white. King squinted to see her this way. The screen door slammed behind them, and John Shire hobbled toward them, the orange tip of his cigarette bobbing, boot scraping the asphalt.

"John says for you to watch after the kid till we get back." *Rose.* Until that moment King had forgotten her, asleep in the front room, beneath the open window. In a minute, Red would take off with John Shire, and Rose would awaken to the ragged, broken roar of the car's ruined exhaust. She would awaken and look out and have to see that—her father pulling away, leaving her. King trotted toward the house, the coins in his pockets ringing, and cut his path to bump John Shire with his shoulder. He wanted to knock him down, delay their departure, but instead caromed off the hard angles of the man. Shire raised his crutches and shifted to keep his balance. Inside, King shook Rose awake.

"Honey, get up, please." Outside, John Shire and Red leaned in toward one another; King followed the glint of her wedding band, her left hand on the car door handle.

"What's wrong?" Rose asked, her voice thick with sleep.

"Nothing, sweetie, we're going to watch a movie."

"Will you tell me a movie?" The car door swung open, and the interior light cut the dark.

"Yes, I'll tell you one. Let's hurry." He took her hand and guided her through the kitchen, up the back stairs to the projection booth. The booth was soundless, and King realized the noise of the exhaust would still reach them with nothing to drown it out. He yanked away the tarp and clicked on the projector. The motor whirred, belts squeaked, and beneath the noise of it King heard the grumble of exhaust. For sound he clapped his hands. Rose looked at him, sleepy-eyed.

"How 'bout we watch one?" he said. "See it on the big screen?" She grinned and nodded, clapped with him. He heard the engine grind climb and fall, but he was listening for it, she was not. The thought reassured him. He told her to pick out one from the stack of reel canisters in the corner. As he spoke, he could make out the crunch of tires on the gravel at the end of the lot.

John Shire steered onto the road, working the levers and ropes that controlled the car. Red let her hand rest on his leg, teasing the inside of his thigh. The mis-pointed beams of the car illuminated part of the road, the tops of trees off to the side.

Rose handed King the second reel of *Swiss Family Robinson*. He fired the projector lamp and aligned it with the screen; a truncated cone of dust floated over the lot, over his Olds still parked and tethered by the curly wire to the speaker post. Rose stood on tiptoe, watching. "Here we go," King said to her.

The Nova turned off the dirt road in a moonlit billow of dust, the taste of which Red had already forgotten. John Shire manipulated the ropes and steering wheel, guiding her to something new. Her mind could be no more specific than that; new, she thought, is good enough. They entered the twisted part of the state road, her eyes following the slice of it lit by their headlights, the car moving swiftly through the curves. *Away,* she thought, *New.*

The gears and belts of the projector clicked and hummed, the perforated edge of the thirty-five-millimeter celluloid fed into the machine as King and Rose followed its path. They watched the shiny tag of film as it worked its way through, obeying the twist and turn of gears that would guide it out the other side where it could be loaded onto the bottom reel, primed then to give them a story—something mindless and happy they both waited to see.

EAT

MY father sat on one of the green revolving stools, stopwatch in hand. The cardboard sign on the door of our Tast-T-Cup Diner, flipped to CLOSED, split the sunlight streaming in. It was Sunday. My mother stood at her spot beside the small, gray cash register, behind the glass case displaying Beechnut packs and cigars, souvenir thimbles and plastic pocket combs. Spatula in hand, bound in a fresh apron, I waited at the grill.

"Ordering," my father said. "Two hard-fried, browns, wheat sliced, side-a-strips torch 'em, short stack and grits. *Go.*" He clicked the watch. I cracked two eggs in one hand and let them plop on the grill, pushed bread in the toaster, threw diced potatoes and bacon behind the eggs, dolloped three puddles of batter the size of saucers and turned them when they bubbled. The bacon made a sound like rain. Toast popped up and I pushed it down again, wet my brush with melted butter as I flipped the eggs, turned the bacon, stirred the pot of grits, shuffled the hash browns. Grease spatters stung the backs of my hands as sweat ran down my forearms and hissed away on the grill. I reminded myself of the man on Ed Sullivan, spinning plates on sticks, not letting any fall. Everything smelled done at once and came together on two blue-edged plates I slid under my father's nose. He clicked the watch and looked at it.

"It don't beat your old man's best," he said, "but damn good enough." My mother smiled.

* * *

Today my father lives in Seven Springs Village, which the brochure termed a *permanent recuperative facility*—a nursing home. We had to send him there following his stroke, a year after my mother passed away. Every Christmas, Jackie and I strap Danny and Lisa in the car to make the trip back to North Carolina. Along the way, I find the places I like to stop for food: Jan's House, Chick and Ruth's, 421 Motor Lodge, and a corrugated tin place near Dover simply named EAT. Jackie, a distance runner when she's not teaching, will order nothing but salad for herself, and plain oatmeal for Lisa (Danny, eight months old, is still nursing). She tells me the place named EAT should be renamed CHOLESTEROL. I tell her it is not the food I go for, though the food is wonderful—chicken-fried steak, green beans from the can, lemon meringue pie with an ocean of egg whites up top.

I go to these places because when I walk through the door

I can smell my father's Dutch Masters Perfectos and Old Spice mixed in the grease and coffee. Now, at Christmas, the windows of the diners carry twinkling strands of colored lights behind the fogged glass; fake-snow aerosol spray spells out "Merry Xmas" across the door. I remember spraying those words myself, T-shirt held over my nose against the fumes. We sit in the vinyl booths, and I do fork and tooth-pick tricks for Lisa, feed quarters to the tableside jukebox. Jackie eats her salad and steals bites of my pie, lets me stay and linger over bottomless cups of bitter black coffee.

* * *

My father tucked the stopwatch in his shirt pocket, drew out a cigar, jammed it in his mouth. He scraped food from the plates onto the cement outside the back door, where stray dogs came to eat the scraps he left out.

"Now," he said. "What do you say to the egg man?"

"Stack 'em, don't crack 'em."

"Good. The bread man?"

"Fresh stuff, off the bottom. No day-old."

"Right-o. Sandy will work the register. She'll be here to help if you get stuck on anything." Sandy was a copper-haired waitress with wiry, muscled arms, deep wrinkles, and black horn-rimmed glasses.

My father pointed his cigar at me. "And if Joe Whelan comes around?"

I gathered up my apron to wipe my hands, a movement learned from watching my father. "Don't serve him any food," I said.

"That ain't all." My father drew a kitchen match from behind his ear, sparked it across his pant leg, sucked fire into the cigar. The smoke stung my nostrils. "The other thing is, throw him out on his sorry ass."

My mother slapped his wrist with a dish towel and told him to watch his mouth. "Just mind the list, honey, and you'll do fine," she said to me.

The list had been made up by my father, scrawled in grease pencil on a piece of shirt cardboard and taped to the side of the cash register:

1. Shirt and Shoes Required.
2. No Money Left Overnight.
3. No Bad Checks.
4. No Biker Jackets.
5. No Transients.
6. No Profanity.
7. We Reserve the Right to Refuse Service to Anyone.

I read over the faded words as if they were the Ten Commandments. Beside the No Profanity rule, someone—Ray Wilson most likely—had written in "this means you, you sonofabitch."

They were leaving on a food-buying trip, to Winston for cured hams, up along the Blue Ridge Parkway for honeycomb, apples, molasses, and the corn husk dolls my mother displayed under the glass counter. My father made the trip every year, on a Saturday, but this time they had decided to go together and stay for a week. I had turned fourteen, old enough to mind the store while they took a vacation. My father wrote a note to get me out of school.

They left on a Wednesday, during the afternoon lull. My father loaded the station wagon with their bags strapped to the top (to leave room inside for the hams). Up to the last minute, he gave me instructions on what to do in the event of holdups or hippies or broken pipes. While the engine idled, he drew me aside and put his arm across my shoulder.

I stared at the black hairs on his forearm, the dark green anchor tattooed there.

"Napkin dispensers, Jess," he said, and lightly shook me. "Don't forget." He had drummed into me his theory that the quality of a diner could be determined from its napkin dispensers. His dispensers—always full—ran a tight, gleaming line down the counter, like a row of chrome fence posts.

My mother, wearing her white gloves and beaded hat, kissed me. My father shook hands, told me to stay out of his liquor drawer, and honked the horn as they drove off in a stream of white gravel dust.

We lived in a neighborhood of look-alike houses on a narrow blacktop that ran perpendicular to Main Street, less than half a mile from the diner. My father had a talent for imagining disasters—floods, break-ins, gas explosions—and did not want to live far from the Tast-T-Cup. The morning after they left I awoke at four, walked under stars to the diner and cooked my own breakfast, unlocked the door for Sandy at quarter till, flipped the door sign to OPEN at five on the dot. The Westin's Feed Store group arrived first, a circle of grizzled old men in caps who spent their days tracing a path from the feed store to the diner, planning hunting trips they never took, inventing lies for one another. They swallowed plates of grits and scrapple and poached eggs with hash. I kept up with their orders while the Bun-O-Matic gurgled coffee smells beside me. The feed store group, led by Ray Wilson, had their jokes over me—"Look, Teddy Hollins left hisself in the dryer too long, shrunk hisself up." They laughed and blew cigarette smoke in the air. Sandy played their straightman, a role usually reserved for my father. I juggled the grill, steam table, and waffle iron, my arms aching and wooden. We cleaned and cooked till the lunch crowd arrived: men in suits from the bank, women in skirts, a few feed store stragglers. We served the fried chicken special, fried okra, canned corn, masterburgers, and chocolate pie. When it ended, Sandy set her lips in a hard, thin line, the closest she came to a smile.

"You did okay," she said.

At eight-thirty my second morning, the leather strap of sleigh bells on the front door jangled, and Joe Whelan stepped in. A hat snugged down to his eyes shaded his blond stubble of beard and wet mouth. His corduroy coat gave off an odor of kerosene. For as long as I could remember, he'd worn around his neck a shoestring with a plastic shark's tooth attached. As he moved to the counter, the men on the stools buzzed in one another's ears. Joe held out his palm, dotted with pennies, his fingers cracked and cigarette yellowed.

"How much you get for donuts?" he asked. I set aside the spatula and gathered my apron to wipe my hands; the feed store gang watched me closely. No one spoke.

"Two hundred dollars, Mr. Whelan," I said. "Of course, you could write me your personal check." Ray Wilson smacked the counter and laughed, the group around him elbowed each other, grinning and shaking their heads. Joe Whelan stared at me, then curled his fingers around his pennies, slid them into his jacket pocket. "I have no use for this," he said, and pushed out the door.

"His father's boy all over," Ray Wilson said, and reached across the counter to slap my shoulder.

* * *

The trip from New York to North Carolina is a long one, and like all long car trips, it invites thought. While everyone is asleep in various corners of the car, I think about my father, try to imagine how another year of decline has left him. Last year's visit, our first since he had the stroke and we placed him in the nursing home, left me shaken, stunned at how nine months' time could take away his heft, shrivel him, cloud his eyes, ruin his legs. As the white lines move under the car, I try instead to picture him the way he looked in the diner, wide-faced and tanned, lighting cigars or wiping his hands on his apron.

After we arrive in Greensboro, I find my father in his room on the third floor, and I am relieved to discover that the year has changed him only a little; he is thinner, his eyes cloudier. Blue veins are visible beneath his skin. He doesn't stir much, and I spend most of the day in a chair beside his bed, reading magazines, watching game shows. Jackie joins me there after she has found someone to sit with the kids. She squeezes my hand. On the table next to the bed, shoved in among bedpans and a remote control for the TV, is a tiny fake Christmas tree, not more than six inches tall. Every once in a while, my father opens his eyes, mutters something and points at us.

"Dad?" I say. His breath is foul and full of noise. I talk to him about the diner, about all the food we served up. He doesn't respond much. Once, he looks at me and says "business," his fingers shaking, and I come to understand that the decline of the last year has not occurred in his body. When I mention anyone from the old days, he nods quickly and squints, but this has become his response to nearly everything, and I know there is no real memory tied to it.

* * *

I had done a half week's worth of good work I knew would please my father. Sunday morning I got up, slicked my hair, drew on my suit and overcoat, carried my mother's red-letter Bible to church for early service. It was a bright fall day; my black shoes kicked through tatters of blown leaves on the sidewalk. I sat beside Mrs. Mashburn, so word of my attendance would find its way back to my mother. The regular morning service had been given over to "Teen Day." Rick Turner, from my geometry class at the Junior High, stood at the front and played "Amazing Grace" on his Sears electric guitar plugged into a shoebox-sized amplifier. Then came a Biblical skit rewritten in teen slang ("Hey, man," Buddy Greenwell as Jesus said, "cast your nets on the other side and everything will be cool"). I walked home and opened the diner, cooked myself a lunch of chicken steak, gravy, and white bread, then settled in at the grill to ready for the after-church crowd.

The next morning at six, Joe Whelan stepped in behind the feed store group. He stood looking around the diner and fingering his plastic shark's tooth. My eyes stung; I looked down and began scraping the grill.

"Joe T. Whelan, my best, long-lost friend!" Ray Wilson said, baiting me. "Pull up a stool here, Joe."

He sat on the stool, placed his hat on the counter, pulled a crinkled five-dollar bill from inside the hatband and straightened its creases. He'd never before had more than a few pennies in hand; I wondered where he'd come by five dollars. Enough money to buy anything listed on the menu.

"Coffee," he said, "Black." Sandy shook her head at me, and Ray grinned, excited. I rested the spatula on the grill, wiped my hands on the white apron.

"Listen," I said, "Your money's not welcome here. Take your business somewhere else." He breathed through his mouth, the matted ends of his hair quivering like leaves.

"Paying customer," he shouted. "I say I'd like some goddamn *coffee.*" He smacked his hand on the counter, knocking one of my father's napkin dispensers to the floor. The spatula rang against the grill as I yanked it by its wooden handle and drew it up, sizzling with grease, in front of Joe Whelan's face. The ring of metal on metal hung in the air.

"Out. Now," I told him. Over and over I repeated to myself rule number seven, that we had the right to refuse anyone. My hand shook as if the spatula handle were electrified. Joe Whelan backed off the stool and stood frowning, scratching his beard. He spat on the floor. "Leave," I said, then watched him pick up and replace the napkin holder, put his hat on his head, and walk out the door.

During the afternoon lull, I carried an armful of grease-spattered aprons toward the laundromat, uptown. I walked breathing diner smells out of the cotton bundle, bumping into people. As I turned the corner by the cafeteria, I nearly tripped over Joe Whelan. He was on his knees, his head pressed against a newspaper machine. Beside him sat a half-empty bottle of cheap fortified wine with roses on the label, and along cracks in the sidewalk ran a stream of reddened vomit. Joe retched, the plastic shark's tooth tapping his chin, his face as gray and parched as old corn husk dolls. He retched again and brought up a wash of air, then fell on his side and began to shiver. Coins rolled out of his jacket pocket onto the walk—his change from the bottle he'd bought with the five dollars I'd refused not three hours before. My heart shook. I dropped my load of aprons, believing Joe Whelan would die at my feet, that it would be my fault. I pulled him up by his corduroy coat, patched bare in spots, stiff with cold and grime.

"You come with me," I told him.

I led him back to the Tast-T-Cup, propped him on a

stool and got him to swallow black coffee till he stopped shaking and could hold up his head. I pulled a menu off the counter and opened it under his nose.

"Order something," I told him. "Anything." He held the menu in his hands, staring at me.

"Coffee," he said slowly, "Black." I wrote it down. Sandy walked out of the back holding a cigarette.

"What in hell is this?" she said. "It's a can of worms, is what." I ignored her, nodded to Joe Whelan.

"Plate of pancakes," he said. "Lima beans and buttermilk. A hamburger, hunk of pie and a roll. Toast with honey."

I fixed it all, faster than my father had ever fixed anything, and laid it out on three plates before him.

"Eat," I said.

And he did. Mouth nearly level with the counter, shoving in the food with his fork, breathing deeply through his nose as he chewed. He downed two more cups of coffee and the buttermilk; I watched the color and heat return to his face. When he finished, he pushed against the counter, drew a deep breath with his eyes closed. He slapped coins from his pocket onto the counter—eleven cents—and walked out the glass door into the sun. On his way out, he shouted back, "Keep the change." I dropped his dishes in the big stainless sink.

"Black and blue," Sandy said, staring at me through her thick glasses. "Your daddy will beat your behind." She shook her head.

My parents returned with their hams, honey, apples, and corn husk dolls. Sandy kept her mouth closed about what had happened, and I didn't volunteer it. My father roughed my hair and squeezed my bicep, told me I'd take over as head grillman someday. My mother gave me a geehaw toy she bought at the Tweetsie Railroad gift shop. My father showed me how to work it. I rubbed the notched stick; the propellers spun first one way then the other.

* * *

Much of the time, my father cannot remember that Jackie is my wife. When he speaks he calls her Meg, my mother's name. He insists the cafeteria of the nursing home is his diner; his nurses tell me that twice during the past year, before he was confined to his bed, they caught him in the kitchen of the cafeteria, pulling pots and pans out of the racks. I pretend concern, but as I sit in the dim light of his room at night, closed inside the thin curtain with him, I think of how good it would be if he could get out of bed and rough up my hair, he and I could sneak down to the cafeteria in the dark, whip up a few egg sandwiches and short stacks and then stuff ourselves. But by now he is beyond even standing. I never made grillman.

* * *

At the diner, things were soon back to normal, my mother running the counter two days a week, me in school, working weekends and afternoons. Ray and the feed store gang bragged on how I'd thrown Joe Whelan to the dogs. School let out again for Christmas break; I strung lights around the windows, taped a cardboard angel to the inside of the door.

On a Monday morning, out of a cold rain, Joe Whelan walked in. It had been more than two months since I'd seen him. The Tast-T-Cup had a crowd, the men from Westin's Feed, people out early to catch Christmas sales downtown. Joe scraped his shoes on the tiles, drug his hat off his head so it pulled his hair straight down toward his eyes. His eyes bulged, swollen and yellowed. The hat moved in his fingers.

"Pancakes," he said. "Coffee, toast—"

"Get the hell out!" my father yelled from the grill. Grease from his spatula dripped. Outside, rain hissed on the sidewalk. Sandy looked over at me; my face burned, and I quickly rang up the check of a gray-haired lady standing before me at the register.

"Out, Whelan, before I call the law," my father said.

"Sic the young'un on him," Ray Wilson said, grinning. I took a five from the woman, my head down.

"That boy'll feed me. Anything I want." Without looking, I felt Joe Whelan point at me.

"You know this man, Jess?" my father asked me. "He a friend of yours?" I handed the woman her change. My eyes watered.

"Best meal I ever had that boy fixed me."

"Oh, I don't imagine that's true, now is it, Jess?"

The gray-haired lady smiled and pressed a quarter into my hand. "Here's a little something for you," she said. I looked at my father.

"You feed those dogs," I said under his hearing, my lips barely moving with the words.

"Want to feed him, Jess?" He winked at me. I squeezed the quarter into my palm.

"No, sir," I said. I looked at Joe Whelan. "Get on out of here."

The cardboard angel muffled the sound of the sleigh bells as the door swung shut behind him. I dropped the quarter into the pocket of my apron.

* * *

Our way home, we are delayed by trouble with the car, and do not start back for New York till afternoon of New

Year's Day. We said our goodbyes the night before at Seven Springs, where the nurses gave my father a noisemaker and strapped a tiny fireman's hat to his head. At midnight, they brought grape juice in plastic champagne glasses, and Jackie kissed his cheek. I shook the thin bones of his hand, and noticed the anchor tattoo on his forearm has faded away. The nurse whispered to us that visiting hours were long since over, that we would have to leave. My father slightly raised his head off the pillow and looked at me. "Rules," he said, and then tried to say it again. I knew it might well be the last thing I'd ever hear him say.

On the road at dinner time, I look for one of my usual places to stop, ignoring a cafeteria with a sign that promises "Open New Year's," and the bright fluorescence of the fast-food places Jackie points out to me. Jan's House, Sarah's Diner, and Marvin's are closed, dark except for twinkling lights and a lit-up, plastic nativity scene on the counter of Jan's. Dusk turns to night, our oldest begins whining, the baby crying. Jackie draws Danny out of his car seat, opens her coat and blouse to nurse him. I give Lisa animal crackers out of the glove compartment and turn up the heater to lull her to sleep.

"Please," Jackie says. "Can't we stop for a burger?" She sounds angry and tired. I don't answer her but keep driving, my own stomach pangs deepening. I pass the golden arches, Burger King, and the others with their blinking signs advertising drive-thrus open till three. Of all the things my father taught me to hate, first among them was fast-food restaurants, which in his mind closed us down. When the first fast-food burger stop was put up in town—a red and white tile prefab assembled in pieces off the backs of trucks—my father stood on the sidewalk across the street to watch the construction, smoking and spitting flecks of tobacco off his tongue. He stood there till dusk. The Burger Palace, as it came to be called, was not built on Main Street, with my father's diner and the other restaurants, but right among the houses in our neighborhood, where Mr. Corgison's place had been torn down. I could see my father through our living room curtains. He stood watching until long past the time the workers had left. His cigar, I noticed, had gone out.

"I know you don't like McDonald's," Jackie says, interrupting my thoughts, "but would just one time kill you?" Danny makes small sucking sounds.

I remember a cardboard sign inside EAT: *Open 24 Hours a Day, 365 Days a Year.* But the diner is outside Dover, still more than seventy miles away. I look at Jackie in the dim light. She rests her chin atop Danny's head, her eyes watery and dark-circled. In a small voice, Lisa says, "Daddy, I'm still hungry." The road we are on runs past another strip of fast-food joints; I turn the wheel to steer us into the parking lot of one.

Through its glass front the restaurant is a loud mix of yellow and red plastic, cardboard clowns dangling by strings from the ceiling, a stainless steel counter lined with computer registers and inflatable Santa Claus dolls. My father would despise it.

I think of what I will miss not stopping at EAT—the inside full of grease and steam, waitresses sliding past in slippers and white nurse shoes, old men with their shoulders bent over the counter, the smell of my father's Dutch Masters and Old Spice. Reflections off the yellow plastic shine through the windshield, illuminating the shadowed faces of Jackie with Danny held close, Lisa sleepy-eyed in the back seat. I shut off the car and sit, hearing the engine tick. Such simple things I long for—warm food and hot, bitter coffee. Jackie looks up and smiles, her eyes full of the easy gratitude that hunger allows.

"You're disappointed," she says. I shake my head. Now seems like the right time to stop. It's late, and we're all hungry.

The Singing Trees of Byleah, Georgia

OUTSIDE her house Etta Cayce wears her tattered housecoat without its matching slippers. She is naked except for the housecoat, the open front of it parting and snapping with the breeze. The housecoat and slippers were the last gift from Garrett, in the year before he put the gun in his mouth and ended his days. She remembers that he wrapped the present in butcher paper sealed with freezer tape, that when she modeled the housecoat for him, twirling the silky blue-green folds around her, he laughed and chased after her calling *chickie chickie*—the name he gave the dozen peacocks that roosted in the trees of their yard.

Etta drags the plastic bucket of kerosene out from the

crawl space and hauls it to the side yard. She breaks through the paraffin covering the kerosene, dipping in deep with her soup ladle while rotted crabapples squeeze up through her swollen toes. The sounds of the trees start up, so to shut them out Etta sings the best song she ever knew straight through, "Dream a Little Dream of Me." She brings up the ladle of kerosene and throws it high into the top branches of the trees. Ladle after ladle she flings in the air, the kerosene raining in drips, filling the air with its oil smell, the smell of their boy, Garrett Junior, long ago sent home from school. She remembers a note he carried from the school nurse, bending him at the sink, pouring the kerosene over his scalp and scratching it in with her fingernails.

She ducks to go inside the trees, the canopy they make above her thick as brocade, their greeny tops woven by the honeysuckle and kudzu that have taken over her yard. All around her are the crabapples, each with a small, perfect bite cored out and then discarded, the birds not liking bitter fruit. The last of the kerosene in the white bucket, the last inch black with dead insects, she pours out in tiny rivers around the roots of the five biggest trees, the ones Garrett planted first, before they pushed him to put the pistol in his mouth. Drips of kerosene fall on her yellowed feet, soreness growing in her joints. Red ants scatter in the path of the tiny rivers. The air under the trees is cooler, like a room with the shades drawn.

The wind thickens and she hears the trees lift their voices, a church choir humming in the rustle of leaves, children singing in far off rooms. She still holds in her mouth like hard candy the best song she knows . . . *Say nightie-night and kiss me.* . . . She shakes as she pulls the matches from her pocket and opens the box. The leaves of the trees shine in the dim light with the oil of the kerosene, the smell heavy in her nose.

The match flares in a whip of light and there is Garrett home from Japan and smoking cigarettes, Lucky Strikes folded in the arm of his T-shirt. Something new he picked up, the way he picked up not sleeping at night, staying awake to watch after the darkness that surrounded the house, sitting on a stack of newspapers in the middle of the dark kitchen with a wet towel on his neck, his pistol held in his lap. This new Garrett who came home, his arm and chest muscles hardened, his skinny sideburns graying, his jokes all wiped away like chalk from a slate. Nights in bed when he stayed soft in her hand.

The match burns down toward her fingers, her swollen joints, and she tosses it, the whispers of the trees finding their way in through the end of her song. *He is, he is.* She recalls a time when she could not hear the voices of the trees, the year the reporters came, the TV men with their cameras and microphones. Somewhere in the house is the article from *Southern Travel* magazine, "The Singing Trees of Byleah, Georgia." She thinks of the Catholics from Atlanta arriving in church vans to hear in the sound of the trees the voice of the Holy Mother, the voice of miracle. Even now Etta sees their hopeful pilgrim faces, the withered priests and nuns, the pink-eared boys, girls in plaid skirts. All grown now, she thinks, the old ones dead.

Flames rise at the base of the biggest tree, climb the trunk quick as a squirrel, heating her long, iron-gray hair. She walks out of the canopy of trees into bright sunlight, back toward the house, the trees' sound like the murmur of a crowd, voices at a train station. *Where is it?* she hears them whisper, their words always nonsense to her, like street corner drunks, arm in arm.

On her porch she turns back to them, hearing the crackle of green wood. "Why *crab*apple?" she asks. Her face is wet, her hands oily with kerosene. For a time the trees gave back to Garrett what it was he lost in the Pacific, brought him out of himself for the six years the trees grew before bearing fruit. His plan was to turn their acre of side yard into a tiny orchard of fifty trees. The saplings he planted on weekend mornings in October, the days edging toward cold, Garrett kneeling in the grass, smoking while he worked, digging out the dirt with a wooden spoon from her kitchen, tamping it down with his fist while ashes shook across his shirtcuffs. When he finished he stood behind her on the porch and curved his dirty hands around her waist.

"McIntosh apples, Etta," he said. "Right in our own yard. You ought to learn how to make apple butter and apple jelly and apple fritters." He spoke quickly. "Think apples," he said.

"Right now?" she asked. He laughed like he'd just remembered how, and rubbed the fronts of her thighs through her dress. "Give yourself about six years," he spoke against her neck, "then we'll have fruit."

Six years till the fruit, she thinks, pulling her housecoat closed. Like he set an alarm clock. And the echo of the pistol's slap still rebounds through these low hills.

Etta scrubs her hands with borax to take away the kerosene. She moves toward the phone to dial Garrett Junior, away somewhere in Chicago or St. Louis. She remembers Garrett telling her once during a phone call from Japan that the words he said took over a minute to travel around the world. That by the time she heard them he was saying something else she hadn't yet heard. That's how it has been since he died, like she is waiting for the next thing he said to get around to her.

She lifts the lace priscilla curtains to see the blaze, to see that it is not nearing the house, if the neighbors have gathered around. In her yard stands a teenage boy hitting the fire with his flannel shirt, stomping it with his boots. A pitiful fire of brown smoke growing in curls away from the shag grass under the trees. The trunks of the trees are only scorched. With her knuckle Etta raps on the windowpane.

"You stop that," she shouts, her words fogging the glass. The boy wears sunglasses on a string around his neck, a red bandanna tied to his thigh. He chews on a plastic drinking straw and looks up to wave.

"You let that fire go," she says, and raps with her knuckle until the windowpane is shot with cracks. The boy lifts tiny headphones from around his neck to his ears and waves again, then gives an okay sign with his fingers. The fire now is only thin smoke, like steam from a kettle. The boy has a red pushcart standing parked in the road, piled up with a lawn mower, hoes and rakes, post hole diggers, hedge clippers, all thrown together and tangled around with garden hoses. He takes a shovel from the cart and tosses gravel from her driveway to cover the last of the fire. Then he gathers his tools on the cart, his head bobbing with the music she can't hear. On the back of his cart is pasted a bumper sticker dirty with oil, but even this far away she can read what it says: MAKE A FRIEND, BUY A HOT TUB, with a picture of two alligators relaxing in a tub. Garrett always said how her gray eyes were sharp as baling hooks. She thinks of a time in the Chrysler on the road toward Biloxi when out the window, twenty feet off, she saw two dragonflies hooked, flying together blue and silver, keeping up with the car while she tried to point them out to Garrett. Now she watches the boy toss his shovel back among the pile of tools and push off down the road with his cart, one of its wheels wobbly on the packed dirt. She can see the sound it would make.

"That's *my* fire," she says after him. "I got a good mind to call the police." She follows him with her eye until he disappears back up on the main road.

Later she lifts the lace curtains again and finds the trees in the evening light, swaying with the wind. The five biggest are black up their trunks in shapes like fingernails. She thinks of the couple who was married inside the trees and wonders how they get along now, how their kids turned out. And she thinks of Madam Velda, who stood in the trees wearing her blond wig, her eyes closed, the police with her because she had promised the trees would tell her where a missing boy was buried, and how later the police had found him in a swamp grave clutching a basketball, his legs gone. Of scientists from the state school on the nightly news, explaining the voices in the trees as "audiological illusion," a phrase she held onto and used for herself, not knowing its meaning. Of Garrett dying before the trees found their voice, before the kudzu and honeysuckle wove a room to occupy the side yard. She thinks of his hands yellow with the crabapples crushed in his fists.

For weeks Garrett had watched the blossoms and then the fruit, thinking something had discolored and stunted them, some disease or blight. He'd already built the press for apple cider and apple butter, bolted it together from her dining room table and the parts off old lawn mowers and bicycles. He bought the peacocks and let them roost in the trees—to eat the bark beetles, he told her, when she knew he really bought them for her. When they cried at night he came to bed and slept, as if their sounds of helplessness gave him peace. He bought farmer clothes from Sears & Roebuck and a kit with which to make apple wine, and he gave up looking for the pistol she'd hidden, the way a child will suddenly give up needing a stuffed bear.

Etta walks out at night into the deeper dark of the trees, the air ripe with humidity and the sound of frogs. When the frogs move under her feet she imagines the crabapples alive, hopping around the yard, struggling to return to the tree, to their blossoms, to fold themselves into their becoming and work back out again as the McIntoshes they were meant to be—juice-filled, shiny-red, weighing down the branches and Garrett there in his Sears & Roebuck clothes to harvest them.

A wind starts with the smell of storm in it and quiets the frogs. The trees say *he is, he isn't,* arguing some point among themselves. Then come the voices and no sense in them, like ten radios playing in ten different rooms. *There's more,* she hears, pushing down in herself the urge to ask anything of them, like the Atlanta Catholics asking guidance, asking grace. She shouted through her screen door at the ones that came: "Those're *trees* you're talking to. No account crabapple trees, trash trees." She became a local character, filler on the wire services, wanting nothing but for everyone to leave her yard. Her picture ran in the back of *Life* magazine; "Miz Cayce," as they called her, smirking at the crabapples through her shiny glasses, quoted as saying "I don't see what all the fuss is about," words she never said, words that only sounded like what someone who looked like her in the grainy picture, someone named Miz Cayce, would say. The neighbors dropped off extra copies for her to keep, which she burned in the fireplace, praying with the gassy green flames curling the shiny pages that she was not really how she saw herself—as the punchline to the joke that had put the gun in Garrett's mouth.

If the trees would only tell her something she could understand. She listens, not singing her song, the one that comes without her thinking it when she steps outside. She touches the trees, the smooth bark. She is listening now, her song put aside, hoping to hear the name of the man who sold to Garrett for a dollar and a half each the trash trees he must have dug up out of some roadside ditch. Garrett stands in the narrow shade of the man's truck while she is home trying again to hide his pistol. Garrett has stopped to buy apples, a sack to eat and a sack to cook, and is eating one he has paid for, the juice drawing the chill of the October breeze to his chin. The man rests his foot on the truck gate, tips his hat (he is wearing one, she knows this, wrapping her arms around the tree, the bark pulling holes in the silk of her housecoat). *Ain't hard to grow 'em,* he says. If the trees know anything, they know his name. Garrett nods and bites while she buries the gun in a shoebox of old letters under the bed and the man figures a price on trees that in six years will bear fruit even the birds won't eat. Garrett sees plans form, feels his mind reverse and begin to look forward to the time of apple pies and fresh cider and apple butter put up in Mason jars, and he takes out his money clip while she places a pair of shoes on top of the box of letters containing the gun on the floor beneath the bed. He loads the spindly saplings wrapped in burlap into the trunk of his Chrysler, already not needing the gun so much or the nights in the dark kitchen of the house. The gun's hid for good this time, she thinks, away from his not needing it for six years until the day came and he found it as if he'd known it was there all along.

She rubs the burnt part of the tree, feels the black rubbing off on her hand. The trees align their voices to ask, *Where?*—not so much a whisper this time as a moan, the wind stronger now. Always it's nonsense she hears, always these questions not tied to anything, like the ones asked by the reporters who came for those months when the trees first started up, when the boys in the neighborhood playing hide-and-seek first heard them and ran home to tell their mamas and daddies. For that whole first year she couldn't hear them, really *didn't* know what all the fuss was about, and just wanted everyone to leave her to Garrett's memory. Now the wind comes heavier and then the rain sounding in thumps on the roof of leaves and branches. She says "audiological illusion" out loud, the words empty, just something she says back to the trees. The thumps sound louder and mushy, a hailstorm outside, the ground inside the trees still dry. *Etta,* the trees whisper, then *Garrett,* twining their names like kudzu vines. She is scared, hearing the names, hearing them as clearly as words whispered over her shoulder when she sits in the church pew. She tries to find the words of her song but has mislaid them, the way she mislays potholders and letter openers. She notices she is cold and draws the housecoat tighter around her, the belt another thing long since lost. The balls of ice punch through the branches above her and make a short hop at her feet, as big as the crabapples, faintly blue in the dark. The rain finds its way in behind the hail and wets her, and she stands up next to the trunk of the tree to let it shield her. She remembers the peacocks shrilling in the lowest branches of the trees, their tails sweeping patterns in the dust at the base of the trunks. *Soon,* the trees say, and Etta finds her song and fills up her ears with it, lets her housecoat drag in the mush of rotted crabapples around her feet.

* * *

By morning she has dried off, sleeping on the porch. Waking, she laughs at herself: an old woman without enough sense to put herself to bed, without enough to come in out of the rain. After a while the boy comes along the narrow blacktop, smoking a cigarette, wearing his headphones and bandanna, pushing the cart loaded with a lawn mower and a red gas can sitting on top, his shoestrings tangled around his feet.

"Garrett, you tie up those strings right off before you crack your head," Etta shouts, startled at the sound of her voice, how like someone else she sounds. The boy slows and looks at her, still walking. She thinks of Garrett Junior all grown in the city with its sirens over the phone, and this one just a boy yet, not war age even. Sleeping in wet clothes in the out-of-doors, not eating the food the county woman brings. She is cutting right through her good sense. When she waves, the boy pushes the cart into her drive. He is all in black, his T-shirt and dungarees, a hat turned around the wrong way on his head. Boys not knowing how to wear clothes proper! Garrett Junior is wearing his old wool suit, pulling at the starched collar while the preacher says his words over Garrett. The police are at the house, still trying to find fragments of bullet, shaking their heads over the peacocks in the absence of their cries while Etta cries at the graveside not feeling it, looking the way she is expected to look, as she will do for the *Life* photographer at a time still twelve years off from this graveside, a time of not-apples, she thinks, watching the boy crush out his cigarette away from the gas can, a time of not-cider, of not-Garrett. Garrett Junior turning away finally when the first shovelfuls fall on the copper and the old Negro men are talking baseball scores while they work, after he has seen her pay the preacher five dollars, and already in his mind are the seeds of his leaving—not to college or vo-tech as she and Garrett had always hoped, but away in the night seven years later in his daddy's car, its tires gone soft from parking so long. She never blamed him for leaving behind any of it, but he must have always thought she did. And now this boy the age he must have been then, that night he left or the day at the graveside tugging his collar in the suit that needed the sleeves let out a little. But everything runs together and she can't remember.

"You need work done, lady?" he asks. "Your grass needs mowing bad," he says, then looks away. Etta looks down at herself and pulls closed her housecoat.

"If you got a saw I'll pay you to cut down these trees." She can't remember if this has occurred to her before, to cut them down. Police took the hatchet and never brought it back to her. She wonders if this boy can hear the trees, what they might say to him.

"*These* trees?" he says, as if in answer to her thoughts. He straightens his ball cap, red lightning bolts machine stitched on the front. "When I was a little kid we called those Spooky Woods. Everybody thought you was a witch or something."

"Well, they don't mean a thing to me. Trash trees." She lifts her chin and reaches for the missing belt on her housecoat. She closes her eyes to see herself all the ways others see her: *Miz Cayce, the witch, the old crazy lady.*

"There's a bunch of 'em anyhow," he says, scratching his head under his hat.

"Two dollars apiece," she says, trying to remember if there is any money in the house. She thinks of the blue-glass tobacco jar in the kitchen where Garrett stored away his dollars for six years, saving to buy more land for more trees, and how for six years Garrett Junior stole out of the jar, she the only one knowing it and never telling, never letting on, like it was some secret conversation between them. After the gun in Garrett's mouth she put the money in still, and still he took it for the seven years until he left, but during that time it never meant anything, a secret kept from no one.

The boy rummages the cart to find a chain saw and starts it up. She watches him bend and guide the saw (slowly, as if he is leading a dance partner) into the base of the first tree in the staggered row. The saw deepens its noise, spitting out white chips and blue, lingering smoke, the chips covering the boy's shoulders and the hair that sticks out from beneath his cap. When he is almost through the first trunk the saw screeches, kicks back at the boy, and dies. The silence that follows whistles in Etta's ears.

"Hit a damn knot or something," the boy shouts. He shrugs, and the sawdust falls from him. She remembers now, like water unwaving itself. Garrett coming through the door with the tiny crabapples crushed in his fists, his mouth gaping as if his words have fallen out of it. She knows the smell of crabapples—a sticky-sweet molting—from her girlhood, as she knows it now mixed in the smell of chain oil, as she has known it always, as if by chance alone it is the odor of her living. Garrett says nothing, but rubs at his face as if to wipe away tears that won't come, smearing the jam of the crushed apples in his red beard. She has to remember back to think of the gun still hidden under the dusty shoes in the box of letters on the floor under her bed. Her first thought is *Where are the McIntoshes?* but then she understands that they are not anywhere, that what Garrett had bought from the man on the same day she hid the gun was the absence of McIntoshes. He walks out through the back of the house, flies swarming at the crabapple mess on his face. She hears bellowing from Garrett, then hears the hatchet he bought to prune back the branches of his apple trees in winter as it hacks chunks from the mahogany of her dining room table, the apple press that he'd made from it. He walks back in, his hand bloodied with the gash from the hatchet. Without speaking he is out the front door and into the orchard. She makes the front window just in time to see him grab the first peacock he comes to and drag it by its tail from the low branches of the apple tree, put his boot on its neck and hack the bird in half. He tosses the tail into the yard while the bird twitches under the tree. He takes them one by one, in the calm of work, as if he *is* pruning branches. They screech and flap, then are caught by the blade, their noise hacked off just as sudden, their iridescent tails tossed away like sheaves of winter wheat.

Ten of them dead in the thin shade of the young trees, then Garrett stops and turns to look at her looking at him through the window, where it seems she has stood for six years, waiting for this to happen. He is dressed in blood, the bits of feathers shimmering green like sequins along his arms. She is glad to God then for Garrett Junior not home, for the school she knows he has skipped with the money he has stolen from the tobacco jar to play pool or watch movies in town, and she knowing for these six years and not telling. She thinks of telling Garrett now, reminding him of what he'd given up or lost in Japan, that his place is at the head of a family and not at the head of an orchard, that there is discipline to hand out. That boy, he'd say if she told, and smile admiring the trouble a son will find. When Garrett starts toward the house he is running, the hatchet loose in his hand. She steps onto the porch wearing the housecoat he had bought her when he was happiest about his apples, silk and blue-green, Garrett telling her in nighttime whispers it was the kind of present he should have brought her from Japan—the kind the other men brought to their wives and girlfriends—if only he could have found his way out of his sadness to do it. She opens her arms to him and then sees the hatchet and the emptiness in his face, and in that moment all her muted love for him is bubbled out by fear, and she turns so that the belt of the housecoat catches on a nail on the porch rail post and tears loose, slipping its loops. She runs in through the house and hides herself behind the wingback chair in the den. She hears Garrett crawl under their bed, hears him find the box, and in the silence that follows she knows that he is tossing her letters one-by-one across the quilt on the bed, their sound almost silence, like the sound of snow hitting the windowpanes, and she knows then that he is gone already and that this tossing of the letters, not tearing them, not throwing, is the last gentle thing he will do. In the noise of the singing of the trees what has not been kept, not sung nor said, is the sound of the pistol shot, its edges softened by palate and cheek and closed lips—a noise long since let go, scattered and blown away like papers caught up in a windstorm.

The doorbell rings and Etta thinks of Garrett home from war, no telegram or letters to warn her, ringing the bell of his own house as if her not answering it would send him away. *Silly Garrett,* she says when he walks in with his duffel bag and sunken eyes, Garrett Junior climbing his legs while Garrett's arms remain stiff at his sides. She opens the door and the tinny voice that comes from her says again *Silly Garrett,* while the boy in the red lightning hat, his face powdered with wood, wipes the sweat from his neck with the back of his hand.

"They're cut," he says, "but they're not down." He blows

his nose into his fingers, and his fingers pull away bloody. "Saw kept kicking on me," he says.

Behind him she sees the crabapple trees tall against the sky, their leaves full of voices, the five blackened trunks.

"I'd like you to take down those trees," she says. Every word in her mouth feels old, some made thing not of her throat. "Two dollars a tree," she says.

"Ma'am, I *cut* the damn trees. Kudzu's got 'em all strung together and they won't fall. Just leaning a little. I'll need rope and my truck to pull 'em down."

She looks past him at the trees leaning in toward the middle, huddled together, the whites of the wedge cuts shining in their trunks like crescent moons, one after the other.

The boy turns his hat back around the wrong way. "I'll get on it first thing tomorrow, but I'd like to get paid first."

She goes for the money in the blue tobacco jar, Garrett saving it up, Garrett Junior spending it on candy and Cokes, pool halls and nights away. The jar is not there on the hutch where it always sat in the kitchen. She comes back to the boy and the trickle of blood runs thin into his mouth. He swipes the blood across his face.

"You don't have my money, do you ma'am?" he says. He shakes his head and snuffs, spits across the porch rail. In his sweat is the smell of the crabapples.

"That boy," she says, and after a minute realizes she's forgotten to shake her head and smile at all the trouble he's caused.

The boy mutters to himself, wipes his head on his forearm, and reaches toward her. She opens her arms, thinking of Garrett reaching for her that first night after the trees were in the ground, the burlap and twine left piled on the roof of the Chrysler. Reaching for her after a year of nights in the kitchen, sitting on a stack of papers and watching the darkness drag the house into night. Reaching and slipping the robe from her shoulders, weighing her small breasts with the tips of his worn fingers, grazing her nipples with his thumbs.

The boy tugs the frayed edges of her housecoat to pull it closed. "Just keep yourself covered up, ma'am," he says, "and we'll call it even."

She hears his boots on the gravel drive as her arms lift away from her like balloons set loose by a child. Garrett lifts her from the floor, her thigh scraping his belt buckle, the smell of outdoors in his hair. Her robe sticks to the sweat on his stomach as he lifts her away from him and onto their quilted bed.

"We're apple farmers, Etta Cayce," he whispers. "How the hell do you like that?" He smiles touching her; the hatchet he has bought to prune the branches that have not yet grown hangs in the workshop, the blade he has whetted and then coated with oil to keep away the rust until the time that he will need it. He kisses her along the length of her body, his Sears & Roebuck clothes soaking in the basin to take the stiff out of them, the sapling trees stretching their roots into new soil, the man in the hat riding off somewhere counting his money, the peafowl not yet hatched on the ranch where Garrett will buy them out of a magazine. The gun is hidden, this time for good, she thinks, beneath the bed where she opens herself to him and he moves on top of her. Above her where she lies, the trees lean in, the holes in the green letting in the failing light of evening. She hears sounds, music, shaken from the branches. Garrett moans, the sound of it like sap running out of the trees; she hears babies crying with new-cut teeth, Christmas music from school assemblies, the sirens where Garrett Junior lives, the Atlanta Catholics praying their rosaries, dogs caught in raccoon traps, wrestling broadcasts on the radio, peafowl in the trees at night, their tails whisking the dust. She hears her song, "Dream a Little Dream of Me," stolen right away from her. *I don't see what all the fuss is about,* she thinks to say. Her hands find the crabapples, one bite missing. Her housecoat lies twisted around her; she needs to find that belt, to close it up tight. She thinks of herself while the noise of the trees swirls around her, *Miz Cayce, that old witch lost out there in the Spooky Woods.* The trees sing to her now. *Blood is falling,* they sing, some old church song, but she won't hear of it, not for a minute. She lifts a crabapple to her mouth for a bite, the bitterest fruit she knows.

Porter's Dodge

PORTER'S knuckles were swollen big as lug nuts, so his fingers hardly worked anymore. He stood at the front window, sore hands braced on the sill, and leaned his nose against the pane, his breath slowly fogging the glass. When he moved, his bones cracked, a sound that put him in mind of broken ball joints. He wiped the window clean to watch the house across the street. Mrs. Burke opened the door and five cats spilled into the yard, then Mr. Burke leaned his large head over his wife's shoulder.

"Me," Porter said aloud to the empty room. "He's looking at me." Burke walked across his lawn toward his red Mercedes parked at the curb, testing its paint for dust as he passed. He continued into Porter's drive; Porter thought to hide his face behind the curtain, but too late—he'd been seen. Burke did a fast lap around the white Dodge ragtop propped on stands in Porter's driveway, shook his head, and mounted the front porch steps. His heavy boots sounded on the boards. A knock sounded, and Porter stepped to answer, his broken shoe flapping the carpet like a flat tire.

"Enough is enough, Porter," Burke said. He stood, hands on hips, dark hair slicked back into a bladelike widow's peak, eyebrows thick and black as a row of birds on a wire. Porter had spoken to him occasionally in the three years the Burkes had lived there. Moving day, before his boxes were unpacked, Burke had come across the street to sell Porter plastic gutter liner.

"The car has to go, Porter," Burke said. "It's an eyesore for the whole neighborhood." Porter tried to remember his last conversation with anyone—Wednesday, the box boy at the store.

"Diesel," Porter said, his throat rattling. Burke looked surprised, the line of birds making a jump.

"Your Mercedes. Runs on diesel. Tough things, engines like hateful women. Never would touch them."

"We weren't discussing my Mercedes, Mr. Porter. Your car doesn't run, hasn't been moved, and it's bringing down my property value. You'll have to have it towed."

"Used to take coffee breaks whenever a diesel came in the shop. Noisy, smelly. You take that old Dodge convertible out there, powerglide transmission, in-line six. She hums, sings tunes, whispers in your ear." Porter rubbed his knuckles.

Burke nodded. "I'd hoped it wouldn't come to this, Porter," he said. "But if you don't move the car I'll call the homeowners' association. I'll call the cops. I mean it."

Porter nodded and extended his hand, wincing when Burke shook it. Burke walked across the street, stopped to blow dust off the glossy surface of the Mercedes, waded through the cats, and disappeared behind his door.

That evening Porter walked, broken shoe flapping, to the Tick-Tock. A pint for his knuckles, to lube them up. Along the road, deep gashes of red clay filled spots where houses had been, new condominiums were planned. On the corner rose a gleaming office park where three years before had curved a gravel road marked by a weedy ditch full of beer bottles. As Porter waited to cross the street, two fire trucks rumbled past. New buildings go up, he thought, old ones burn down.

At home Porter drank from the bottle and pressed his nose to the window. Many nights Burke threw crowded parties, his house lit up, the neighborhood crammed with Japanese and German cars blocking Porter's driveway. Tonight all was quiet, empty. The whole, still house settled around Porter, pressing on him. He drank to thin the blood in his hands, like packing a wheel bearing with fresh grease. He turned his pale hands, stretched them for their fit to a crescent wrench, a pry bar, a feeler gauge.

Porter remembered Burke, his first week there, had said, "Me and the boys," like he'd arrived familiar with everything and everyone in Porter's own place. A football pool was the scam (the word suited him: *scam*) for Burke and "the boys," and did Porter want in? Then baseball, boxing, anything that would hold a bet. Every time, Porter said no. And still, Burke reminded him each visit, Porter's gutters needed lining.

The only bets Porter made were with himself, and most of those he lost. Molly gone, kids scattered—like lottery tries thrown away. The Dodge, on blocks seven years now;

a rebuild needed for something old enough that no one remembered its birth on a Detroit assembly line. No work left in useless knuckles. Porter drank, the amber line a quarter down the label now. His hands numbed. In his fist he gripped the bottle neck like a torque wrench—sixty pounds, ninety; he drank, and pretended to tighten the arms of his chair. Just enough, he told himself, not too much. Drinks piled up in him like weights tipping a scale. Doctors had warned him against it. He capped the bottle, set it on the shelf sideways, like a book.

Outside, Porter traced the lines of the Dodge beneath a blue street lamp. The powdery paint rubbed off like chalk on his hand. Mosquitoes, hatched from rusty pools in the floorboards, sang in his ears before biting. He smelled the mold that laced his upholstery. The bumper held as he lifted himself onto the hood and lay back, pillowing his head with the windshield. When the car was new Porter would lie like this parked on back roads, Stanley or J.C. or Harden beside him, radio playing, a sweaty bottle passing between them. Then into the car, top down, along the black roads that snaked between foothills and, where the hills tapered down, rolled out flat and opened to the sky like a dark carpet unfurled, blacktop paled to gray by a low moon, the Dodge hitting an easy eighty and humming.

He remembered his forty-fifth. "You old now," Harden told him, and they ran the road. That night J.C. drove, and Porter stood on the front seat facing the blast of air, gripping the top of the windshield, riding the jolts that shook him knee to face, laughing, the wind snatching handfuls of his hair. Behind the Highway Six package store they stretched across the hot hood, the still engine ticking from the heat-damp August night—above them, a meteor shower. They watched stars fall, burn out like Fourth of July rockets.

"Somebody's light going out," Harden said. Another star fell: "Somebody else's."

Across the street, Burke passed his bedroom window wearing shiny black pajamas. Mrs. Burke too, her blonde hair stacked up, blue robe flowing around her. Porter watched Burke encircle her from behind and kiss her neck, then cross the window again. The room went dark. Porter felt the white car beneath him like a hard snowbank—cold, sealing an ache in his joints. He rose stiffly. Tomorrow, he would fix the Dodge.

Whiskey in his coffee, enough to loosen his hands. As he drank it down, the door sounded. He opened it to Burke's face.

"Ever hear of the environment, Porter?" Burke said. "The county has regulations. That monstrosity of yours leaks purple liquid all over the drive. Gets in the ground water. Never mind the mosquitoes and vermin holed up in that thing. The county will be here Monday, to investigate. They'll take your damn car away."

"Steering fluid," Porter answered. "One of the first for power steering, real innovation. Not to mention the FM."

Burke smiled. "You just play your little game, Porter. The car's gone. The process has started." Then he left. Porter went inside and drank past what his knuckles needed, the amber line down to the rose on the label.

The toolbox an easy weight in his hand, Porter walked out and paced around the Dodge, lifted its hood. Beneath was rust and cracked hoses, pools of oil like small lakes on the engine block. Atop the water pump sat an abandoned bird's nest. Porter closed the hood, walked to the parts store and emptied his wallet, then to the Tick-Tock where he bought a pint on credit. He borrowed a cart from the Safeway and pushed home with his purchases, drank, and rolled up his shirt sleeves.

Burke, rubbing a fresh shine on the red Mercedes, stopped to watch as Porter laid out his tools.

"It's beyond repair," Burke shouted and laughed, as if sharing a neighborly joke. Porter snapped the seal on the new pint and walked out toward the Mercedes, his legs wooden beneath him.

"You don't know cars, Burke," he said, his voice too loud.

Burke shook a handkerchief from his pocket to polish the three-pointed star mounted on the hood.

"This is a car," he said. "It breaks—I write a check. I know enough." Everything about the Mercedes smelled new. Porter peered inside: brown leather, golf clubs on the back seat, white shoes with spikes on the floorboard.

"A car is born, has a life, dies," Porter said. "It tells you this through your hands."

Burke laughed. "I hope yours tells you bye-bye," he said. "Come Monday, it's gone." Porter drank from the pint, set the bottle on the hood. The wax made the bottle slide; Burke snatched it away.

"You'll scratch the paint!" he shouted. He shoved the bottle at Porter's chest. Burke bent his face to the hood.

"Look. You put a hairline in it."

Porter leaned toward the red hood, wavered, squinted. The surface blinded him, like sun reflected off deep water. Heat from it warmed his face, the paint red as fresh blood, his reflection melted so he could not make himself out. No scratch that he could see. They were quiet. Burke polished the hood.

"So," Porter asked, "how's the football pool?"

"Welcome to July, Porter," Burke said. "No football."

Porter, still bent, searched his distorted face in the surface of the car. He wanted to watch his words spill out of his mouth.

"You're a betting man," Porter said. "I bet I can get my car to run, drive it away."

Burke rubbed the imagined scratch and shook his head.

"By dark, tomorrow," he said, "take it around the block and you keep the damn car, leave it on blocks, whatever. You lose, you pay the towing first thing Monday. Sucker bet, friend."

Porter drank, his hands numb. "Okay," he said, and left Burke polishing the Mercedes.

Porter watered the battery, hooked it to the charger, cleaned the carb jets, replaced all the hoses. Band-aids, he thought, for cancer, for heart disease. When darkness came, Porter fired two trouble lights strung from the house. Beneath their light the broken engine looked startled, exposed. He tipped the bottle to keep his knuckles oiled; a pain began in his side, the scale in him tipping. Beneath the car, on a creeper looking up, Porter cataloged the deterioration. Tie rods gone, leaks from the oil pan, rust blackening everything like a forest fire. He worked, cutting corners, cheating, patching things, as Harden used to say, with spit and prayer.

Near midnight he primed the carb with lawn mower gas, turned the key in the ignition. The starter whirred and shook the frame, the engine wheezed then backfired, coughing up a faint cloud of blue smoke. Rings nearly gone, Porter realized, timing chain bad. He cranked again, another blue cloud rose fragile as a soap bubble. Porter watched it lift with the breeze toward Burke's house, imagined it seeping through Burke's walls, him sleep-breathing it, drawing it into his blood. Then, the carbon smell in him, Burke might understand what Porter understood, what Stanley and J.C. and Harden, all gone, had known. He would let the car stay until the earth took back its iron.

The engine's whirring as he cranked it spoke of its ruin. Camshaft scarred, pushrods closed up like bad arteries. In the heart—the combustion chambers—no strength left, no compression, too much heat. Porter drank and worked—pulled a wrench, leaned into the pry bar—till his hands shook. The line of amber in the bottle shrank to thin as a fanbelt.

Beneath again on the creeper, Porter replaced the front seal and reconnected the steering. His head resting on the slick wood, he grew sleepy. Above him, past the engine well, the black sky full of stars lay like a tarp thrown over the car. His eyes watered, the stars blurred to a white smear, then the car groaned against its jackstands. He snapped awake, remembering that groan from the shop: Cheston Meyers crushed beneath the big Lincoln, how everyone in the garage had identified him by his legs sticking out, by the yellow socks he always wore, before the car had been lifted. Porter shot out from beneath the Dodge, shook the car to test its set on the stands. Squeaks, but no groan, no sick scrape of metal.

The sky shifted from black to dark gray. Thick dew settled on his tools, the car's hood, his pant legs. His fingertips were blue, the knuckles stiff. The amber flowed in him like water. Porter lowered the car, tested the belts with his thumb, knocked dust from the air cleaner. As he bumped the starter to line up the pistons in their cylinders, he felt through the numbing tips of his fingers the car's readiness. He poured gas in the tank. Enough work had been done.

Porter primed the carb, turned the key. The starter

whirred, vibrated, caught. The car jumped, orange flame shot from the carb two feet, a throaty roar shook the ground. Porter moved to slam the hood, swimming a cloud of blue smoke. The Dodge settled to a shaky idle full of grind and scrape. Inside, his feet soaked by the floorboard puddle, Porter shifted to Drive and rolled into the street, his pint bottle a passenger beside him. He hit the accelerator in Neutral; the ragged exhaust note bounced against the houses. With his thumb Porter pressed the horn ring, and a raspy bark swelled from under the hood. Lights came on inside houses, curtains parted. Porter watched Burke's house, still dark, then leaned on the horn again. The bedroom light came on, the front door flew open and Burke ran out in a paisley robe, shouting something Porter could not hear over the grind of the engine.

Porter danced the gas pedal, raced the engine, then hit Drive and scratched away in a burned rubber smell. The car listed hard to the right and he fought to keep the road, ignoring the stop signs. The gauges held; Porter made the right-hand turns that carried him around the block, back down his own street. From the top of the rise he saw Burke, leaning at his porch rail, watching. Burke shook his head and laughed at Porter. He raised his hands and slowly applauded. The process, Porter realized, *had* started: tools rusting, driveway empty, the car already not his. Wager or no, the inspectors from the county would be there Monday. A sucker bet, yes. Burke collected it with his laughing.

Porter shifted to Neutral, imagining Harden, Stanley, and J.C. packed in the car with him, along with Molly and the kids, Cheston Meyers with his yellow socks. The bottle held between his knees, Porter said aloud, "Here we go," coasted the rise, and watched Burke wave his arms. The road dipped. Porter cut hard and slammed the red Mercedes head on. Porter's forehead hit the steering wheel like a window slammed shut. He heard glass spray across the hood, the twist of metal, a hiss of air. Shaking, he lifted the pint in a toast to Burke. The amber line erased, Porter's insides seized him. His vision blurred. He held his stomach, reversed the car and backed away, drove forward again. Metal scraped metal, something behind him dragged the street. The Mercedes sat creased, a shower of tinted glass and red paint chips dotting the folded hood. Burke ran across his lawn, trailing his robe, screaming. Porter levered the accelerator and the Dodge lurched forward, out of the neighborhood.

Porter found the old roads that twisted through the foothills, toward the place where the hills fell away and the road evened to a hard, dark line. He touched the cut on his head, tasted a button of blood and watched the gauge needles dip. A hiss sounded—oil and antifreeze spewed from under the hood and clouded the windshield. Halfway through their arc, the wipers burned out. Porter shifted to Neutral and stood in the seat, steering with one hand. The warm blast of wind pushed tears from his eyes, blew his shirt flat against him, whipped his hair. He coasted, glass fragments rattling in creases along the fender.

As Porter leaned out to wipe the windshield, his eye caught the hood ornament from the Mercedes—twisted, stuck like a wasp in his wiper blade. He grabbed it, tossed it to the floorboard, and watched it sink in the shimmering pool where the pale light of early morning reflected. The Dodge hit eighty, the hills rushed past—an outline of trees, faint moon stuck high in their branches.

Knots

My husband Ray and his cronies are sports—they crush beer cans with their foreheads, stage arm-punch contests, wear identical hula girl tattoos. But their pranks are the worst. I get caught in the middle and it binds my stomach. One year, on Ray's birthday, a policeman knocked on our door and asked to step inside, then stripped down to fuchsia bikini pants and shouted, "Charlie sent me!" Ray chased him away swinging a beer bottle, then made me phone Charlie and ask him, in this nasal operator's voice, to accept a collect call from the Knoxville city jail. (Charlie's son Beau lives in Knoxville, and he's had trouble with the law.)

I know what you're saying, I married him. But that was

ten years ago, and things were different. We met when I turned nineteen, Ray was twenty-eight. Two girlfriends dragged me to a home game of the Winston Hornets, a class AA farm team for the Atlanta Braves. Back then I knew diddly about baseball, but I liked cold beer, shouting crowds, and dusty August nights when the sun stays up past eight. I watched the game in spurts, ate cheeseburgers with onions. On the bleacher before me, two men with shocks of gray hair and fat, splotchy noses jeered at the players, and with every pitch or whack of ball cursed and clutched at their heads. They consoled themselves with rancid cigars and large tumblers of beer. It was Hornets cup night.

Ray pitched that evening. I caught him looking my way when the innings changed, as he walked toward the dugout. The rest of the game he cast his eye toward me more than his strike zone. I wore cut-off jeans, a halter top made from two red bandannas. After the Hornets lost, he walked over carrying his glove and ball. My girlfriends went for the exit.

"You look like that chick from Li'l Abner," he said, a lump of tobacco like a thumb in his cheek.

"You look like that dog from Orphan Annie," I said back. He laughed and whooped and spat, winked at the old men.

"Listen, I'm sweating awful," he said, "mind if I borrow one of those?" He pointed to my bandannas, and I blushed to match them. Even now, a trickle of Baptist upbringing runs in me like a faucet dripping. He asked what I thought of his game. I repeated everything I heard the two old men complain about.

"Your curve broke too soon," I said. "Couldn't find the inside, the slider wasn't working, and your fastball was off." He raised his eyebrows, impressed. Then he turned, pointed over his shoulder with his thumb at the stitching across his back.

"Brower," he said, "Ray."

"Rawlings," I answered, "Charlotte."

"Rawlings? That's the name on this ball." He held up the grass-stained baseball.

"Give me that," I told him, reaching with red-painted nails.

He grinned, snatched it away. "This ball is game weary," he said. "Snagged hide, lopsided. A throwaway." He made to toss it in the trash barrel.

"It's mine," I said, and grabbed it, tucked it safe in my bag. He spat again.

"You're a real queen," he said, and grinned. Let me tell you, in a young man, boyishness is a seductive thing; by middle age it's a tumor on the personality. Three weeks later, we were married.

It's Saturday, and Ray sits home filling out bill-me-later subscription cards for my *Ladies' Home Journal, Redbook,* and *Banking News* (I'm a teller at First Federal). Five-year subscriptions on each, in the name of his best friend, Earl. All because Earl mailed us a giftwrapped box of rotten banana peels and fish heads. I stand at the sink eating an English muffin and doing arm curls with the Sears catalog. Lately, I've been trying to improve myself, and have even looked in the community college listings for a course to take on one of Ray's nights out. Right now it's a toss-up between *Knot Tying For Sportsmen* and *Basic Auto Mechanics.*

I do a curl, take a bite—pain shoots through me like a hot needle, from my tooth straight down my arm.

I keep my head in emergencies. Three years ago, at First Federal, I had just popped on a rubber thumb to begin the final drawer tally for the day, when in walked two men wearing Halloween masks, Casper the Ghost and Spider-man. One of them jammed a stubby pistol in my cheek and told me to fill the grocery sack the other man tossed on the counter. I bent, stuffed in some bills, then a dye bomb, then more bills to cover it. They rolled up the bag, walked out the tinted doors. Channel Five News that night showed police dragging the suspects out of their Vega, which had crashed in a ditch when the bomb exploded. The insides of the car and outsides of the robbers were covered with the red dye, which comes off, the label warned, only when the skin cells wear away. The robbers looked like they'd been turned inside out. The next week, Mr. Tuttle put my picture in the bank lobby with "Hero of the Week" written underneath.

I hold an ice cube to my jaw as I dial the dentist; a recording tells me Dr. Jackson is on vacation, his patients are to be seen by Dr. Neuman. I call his office and he answers, tells me to come right down.

"Ray, will you drive me to the dentist?" I say, trying not to move my mouth.

"Earl's bringing over his remote-control dune buggy," he says. He signs Earl's name to an offer for free information on Eva Gabor wigs.

The pain jumps down my arm again, and I shiver. "I want you to take me, Ray."

"You telling me you can't play injured, Charlotte? Now, be a good girl and don't bite the doctor." He whacks me on the rear. When I look at him, he grins and turns back to his work.

Dr. Neuman's office feels cool, smells of cinnamon mouthwash. Magazine stacks dot the wicker furniture like sprouted flowers, and Beethoven music plays in the background. The doc himself sits at the receptionist's desk. I read his nametag and study his hands, which are spread out over a pile of bills. His ring finger sits empty, which I still have good radar for noticing after ten years off the market.

"Marge doesn't work Saturdays," he says. "You'll have to excuse me." He glances up, and I find myself nailed by eyes blue as the plastic ice blocks that keep beer chilled in the cooler. Back in the examining room, he lowers me in the vinyl chair, points at me the thing that looks like a headlight mounted on a silver tea tray. I see my reflection, the inside of my mouth full of gray fillings. Dr. Neuman bends over me, moves his face near mine; his breath has the same sweet cinnamon smell as his office. Beneath thin hair his scalp glows pink. He isn't dressed like a dentist; under his white lab coat hang faded jeans and a beat-up alligator shirt.

I need a new crown. Dr. Neuman—Alex, he asks me to call him—fits a temporary till the new one can be ordered. He draws novocaine into a hypo, stings my palate with a quick jab. Then he sits and waits for my jaw to numb. We talk about dentistry and oral hygiene, my job at the bank, the weather. Every so often, he reaches up and touches my face, testing for numbness. I ask about the silver tools lined up on the machine beside me, and accidentally spray a stream of water on the green wall. Alex laughs. His thin hair and build are close to Ray's—with a small paunch dimpling above his belt—but he has those blue eyes and a voice that lifts when he speaks, a sound like fresh-hung laundry snapping in the wind.

I want never to leave this vinyl chair—laid back, carrying along my end of the conversation. About the only men I've talked to in ten years are the moon-faced jokers that orbit Ray, all like rowdy school boys on a field trip. As I speak to Alex, the novocaine spreads over my face like sweet cream spilled on a tabletop.

"Do you like sports?" I ask.

"Sailing," he says. "I like the ocean, riding the waves. I make time for it."

He fixes the temporary tooth, smiles, pats my arm.

"Take care of that crown," he says, taking me in with those eyes.

"Thank you," I tell him. "I will."

At home I decide on the knot tying class; it meets only one night a week, on Ray's poker night. As I fill out the application, it occurs to me that knot tying would be useful if I ever went on a sailboat. I tell Ray I've signed up.

"How much?" he asks. "Why in hell do you want to learn that?"

I tell him I will pay from my bank bonus, that knots are a part of everyday life and knowing how to recognize them might be helpful someday. He shakes his head, turns back to his VCR to watch a Braves game he taped two days before. He does that, watches yesterday's games. I couldn't watch a game where the box scores have been posted, cleats hung in lockers, knees untaped, stadium emptied. Old news. Ray will replay Atlanta games three or four times.

"I was almost a Brave," he likes to say. "That close." His cronies eat it up.

Things with Ray got worse when I thought they'd get better: after he quit baseball. When the Braves wouldn't offer him a coaching job, he went to work for Boren Brick, loading trucks. No more playing for a living, I thought, and I was right—playing became a full-time hobby. I lived with the pranks, his buddies, because I thought he would outgrow them—when you plant a bulb, you expect a tulip to sprout up. He quit the team six years ago; I had just turned twenty-three, Ray was thirty-two, too old to play, by then his chance at the bigs something long since behind him, something lost in his youth the way tonsils are removed from children. Since then we've been through twenty-four seasons of the year. I've worked to love him, and he's buried himself in his pranks.

The class meets in a yellow concrete-block room at the YWCA. Our instructor walks in late wearing a noose of thick rope loosely hung around his neck. He rolls his tongue as he tells us his name: Wolfgang Kubler. Wolf, he asks us to call him, wears steel-frame glasses on his wide face; when he speaks strands of gray hair shake across his forehead. He says he worked thirty years in the German merchant marine, and tells us knots are a matter of life and death. His mastery of knot tying came after a badly hitched guy rope securing a lifeboat on his ship snapped, severing his pinky finger down to the first joint. He shows us the stub.

Seven of us are in the class. We have to go around the room and introduce ourselves. Jay and Tim, two pimply boy scouts, sit slumped against the back wall. Next to me grins a young couple, Pete and Marie, camping enthusiasts, they say. Jimbo, an aging-hippie mountain climber, and Robin, my age, strawberry blond and a macramé artist, sit on either side of me. All have some reason to be there, a purposeful interest in knots.

"I'm Charlotte," I say, "Rawlings—like the baseball." Easy as that I bring my old name out of mothballs, as if being called after a baseball gives me some connection with sports and knot tying, some reason for being in a yellow room at the Y while my husband gambles away his paycheck.

Wolf hands out a xerox page with drawings of all the knots we have to learn: dove hitch, carrick bend, Turk's head—a page full. Wolf paces the room in cowboy boots, lectures us with his brick-hard accent. He tells us—stopping to pound the desk—that knots are best learned by untying them, that yanking a hitch gives life to a rope, that good knots are part of a universal design (he whispers this, and points to spider webs in corners of the room).

I cut down an old clothesline strung between two oaks in the backyard, and fill it with blackwall hitches, cat's paws, figure-eights. My drape cords soon hang with bowlines and timber hitches. I knot lamp cords ("Go ahead," Ray tells me, "fry your butt."), shoestrings, loose strands of my own long hair. Ray's friends ask him when he's going to jerk a knot in my tail. I ignore them and keep practicing my knots, tying the house together. Wolf, in our third meeting, explains that knots have purpose, each its own job to do. He teaches us sailing knots, how lanyards pass through deadeyes to extend shrouds. The ocean devours what is not secured, he says, and I shiver to think of Alex out on rough seas without me to rope everything down.

Saturday, I go for my tooth. Alex first fills a cavity that has shown up on the X-ray. He wears a blue work shirt, jeans, boat shoes, and no lab coat. He rolls up his sleeves as he starts to work, showing arms dusted with bleached hair. Again, as the cement sets, we talk.

"I wanted to show you something," he says, then reaches in his pocket and hands me a photo of two hazy white shapes, one large and one small, floating beneath the surface of slate-colored water.

"Beluga whales," Alex says. "Spotted them in the North Atlantic, near Nova Scotia. They must've separated from the herd. Nearly fell overboard taking the picture." A corner of the blue deck of his sailboat cuts into the side of the picture. On it is tangled a fraying rope, lying in a heap. Beyond that, the ocean foams, bitten all over with whitecaps.

Seeing that rough water and nothing but a frayed, tangled rope makes my heart skip. But the whales are beautiful, the pair of them, drifting like clouds just under the water. I want to see one for myself, and tell him so. He laughs, his voice lifts: "Maybe I should take you with me sometime," he says.

"I know knots," I tell him, and tie a quick, tiny bowline in a length of dental floss. He laughs again; a real laugh, shot up out of surprise, not mired in menace like the laughs of Ray and his cohorts. I see how easy it would be to bring Alex along, something I haven't practiced in ten years, how readily I might lean forward in the vinyl chair, touch the wrinkled corners of his eyes, and kiss him. Then the trickle of Baptist in me warms my face.

"You have any kids?" I ask. "A wife?"

He turns dentist on me then—checks my chart, holds X-rays to the light, adjusts the water flow swirling in the spit basin. As he works he gives me his story, how his marriage came unglued after his son, James, died at fourteen months with a heart defect. Alex tells me this matter-of-factly, like a TV show detective. Then he examines my mouth.

"A chip in your front tooth, here," he says. "You might want to consider bonding."

"I might," I tell him. That evening I sit home practicing knots on my bathrobe sash, thinking of those white whales swimming the ocean.

The plastic tube out of the box from the Winn Dixie tells me as loud as a flashing neon sign: pregnant, with child, knocked up. I've had clues to what was happening, so I shouldn't be surprised but I am anyway. Like when the men walked in the bank and took the money—sometimes things sneak in when you aren't looking. Sitting on the toilet with the test kit in my hand, I have one good thought: fatherhood might legitimize Ray's toy buying, his game playing. I think that when I tell him, he might whoop out loud like the night we decided to get married, or pick me up by the waist and dance me around as he did the year the Hornets won the Sally League pennant.

When I sit that night and tell him, whisper it to him, he leans his elbows on the dinette table, rubs the back of his neck.

"I thought you were careful," he says.

My face heats up. "You're wrong, Ray," I say, standing, "I'm not careful, I'm dangerous." I run and lay on the bed, rubbing my stomach, the bundle of new cells inside—what Wolfgang Kubler might call a good knot.

A week later Ray's pals show up drunk on the front porch. They open the screen door, letting in moths and mosquitoes. Charlie, Earl, and the others storm the living room, carrying wrapped packages.

"A baby shower!" Charlie says, "For the man! Get it?" He laughs and pulls out a bottle of Jim Beam. "You get it?" he says again.

They pour drinks into Ray, call him "daddy," and "the old man," slap his back, get him good and drunk. As the guys scream, Ray unwraps his gifts: a doll baby wearing a Pampers full of rubber doggie-doo, Doctor Spock's book with Playboy photos pasted on every page, and, finally, an eighteen-pound boat anchor with a thick chain, the anchor pinned in a diaper. The anchor has them rolling, spilling drinks on the rug. In the midst of it all, I watch Ray look up at the stucco ceiling, shaking his head.

"A baby," he says. "A damn *baby*." He looks more miserable than I've ever seen him.

"An anchor with a diaper!" Charlie screams. "You get it?" Ray nods; he gets it. So do I.

The house is still all evening till Ray says, "Listen," and I prick right up. I've been waiting for this since his friends left. He looks at me, his eyes red and drowsy.

"We don't need a baby," he says. "You ought to have it taken care of." He looks down, trying to balance the salt shaker on its edge. We sit for a while without saying anything. Then I stand up to walk away. "I'll think about it," I tell him.

The next afternoon Ray calls to say he's made the appointment for me. As we speak I clove-hitch the phone cord, and understand that the life we have together is no place to bring a baby. There is a long space of silence while I let the clove hitch unwind itself.

"Ray, could you go with me this time?"

"Hey, no problem," he says.

I take a deep breath. "Okay," I tell him. My voice stretches out thin over the phone wire; when he hangs up, the connection snaps, like the guy rope securing the lifeboat on Wolf's ship, and some small part of me severs.

At the Family Planning Clinic, the nurse gives me forms to fill out, and I sit in the middle of a big green vinyl couch. The couch is empty (Ray, of course, has not come), but there are others waiting there with me. Two young girls, teenagers, sit with their boyfriends (no wedding rings) on orange loveseats. The boyfriends, skinny and pimpled, remind me of the scouts from knot-tying class. The four of them look like movie-goers waiting for the show to begin.

The forms finished, I'm told to wait, and sit again on the empty couch. I pull the venetian blind cord into my lap (the room dims, no one notices), and twist it with my fingers. Tonight is to be my last class at the Y, but given the circumstances, I figure to miss it. I rub at my stomach, the baby forming there, a half-hitch of tissue growing eyes, hands. I think, this is the one good thing to come of us, and I am about to undo it. A dizziness swarms over me, this baby already locked in, changing my chemistry. I close my eyes.

"Are you okay?" one of the teenage girls asks.

"I think so." I lean back into the couch, holding to the thin cord of the venetian blinds. When I open my eyes I see the work of my hands, that with the gray cord I have made a tiny noose, shaped like the one Wolf wore around his neck the first night of class. It isn't a knot we have studied or practiced. I can't see how I have come to know it. The knot is perfectly done; you could hang some tiny doll with it. The thought stirs up nausea and a heat that sticks my skin to the vinyl couch. I feel lost on the couch, pulled down by it. Panic sets in like a steel wire drawn through me. I close my eyes again, think of ten years of my life, stolen away, of these wide-eyed teens, that they have found this much trouble so young. I think about Ray, that he is not here to be afraid for me. Then everything explodes inside me, shaking my heart with one clear notion: I want to keep this baby, my daughter. I untie the noose and yank on the cord, letting in the light from outside.

At home, Ray is watching taped baseball; I run in and undo every knot in the house, Ray saying "What the hell is this?" over and over, a broken record. I don't answer him. With my clothesline empty of knots I leave for my last class of *Knot Tying For Sportsmen,* run to the car with my hand held over my baby. My picture of her inside me is like those hazy white shapes of whales near the surface. I think that some day, when she is old enough, I could take her out to the middle of the ocean with me and someone like Alex, that we could find whales to show her, dozens of them surrounding us, with waves pitching over the sides of the boat, but everything would be tied down secure, and we would all know we were safe, and that none of us could be washed away.

THE EXTENT OF FATHERHOOD

AT night the scrapers come. They rumble like dinosaurs to snatch me out of sleep. I sit up with the goosedown bag damp around my knees, moist hair in my eyes, and lean back with a cigarette against the boardwalk to watch them. Their headlights fire the sand and burn mist from the air; moths circle in the light. Beneath me, the ground quivers with the weight of five-foot tires. The machines feed in pairs on the waste of beachgoers: cups, plastic bottles, abandoned blankets and styrofoam surf boards. They churn and sift the sand, swivel their heads and run shiny with spray. In the dark the ocean is tar, molten, running into a tar sky, surging to melt away beach. The men who work the scrapers are invisible inside the plexiglas cabs. I wave at them anyway, wave at the machines chewing at surf's edge, eating footprints. They follow me like stray dogs. They have a taste for the footprints I leave.

When they go they carry away their rumble, leaving tire ruts and clean sand. The noise of the ocean returns, the string of foam on the breakers glows faint blue in the dark. My fingers burn with the cigarette, and I toss it away. Tired by an ache in my shoulders, I slide inside the bag, settle my head in a cobweb space beneath the boardwalk. My sore joints gorge on sleep.

I have a system in doing things. I am not random, not a hobo or a bum. The Assateague Island National Park lets me spread my bag on swept pine needles and sleep with the sounds of backwater streams, wild ponies scratching through brush. A seven-day limit is imposed; they don't want people living there, where families vacation in pop-up campers. After a week I hitch across the bridge to Ocean City, and sleep up next to the boardwalk where the wind and scrapers can't get me. Shelly's tape deck moves with me. I cart it back and forth between the beach and the campground, listening to the one cassette I kept, Dylan's *Blood on the Tracks*. If the batteries go, I'll chuck the whole thing into the surf.

When I left I took a sleeping bag stuffed full in the toe with winter clothes, the jeans and sweat shirt I'm wearing, the book Shelly gave me. October is here, stirring up overcast days and cold breakers, giving me worry over whether I took enough to wear. The girls in the Dutch Bar have thrown flannel shirts on over their bikini tops. All of the amusements are boarded up with plywood.

Mornings pull me back into bright sky and sweat. Overhead, gulls swirl and float, diving at sand fleas. The beach is not crowded this early in the day, this late in the year. A few old people sweep the sand with metal detectors. Spandex surfers test the waves. I smoke, pull on my shoes, roll up the bag and stash it, turn on my tape and hum along. I appreciate the sound of my voice.

I eat dinner at the Paul Revere. In the waiting area, a young couple take pictures of each other locked head and hands in the wooden stocks. I sit and order tea, then make slow movements around the salad bar, reaching under the plastic guard for cherry tomatoes, chicken wings, captain's wafers. For ten minutes I stuff my mouth, then leave without paying. Dishonesty. Stealing. Not things I would want to teach my boy.

After dinner I end up at the Dutch Bar, spending what I've found that day on the beach, pocket change left on blankets. I lean next to some wiry kid, nineteen or twenty. He reminds me of the boys I used to instruct in my Industrial Welding course at Lincoln Technical College, slouched kids with long hair, black T-shirts. He starts talking about motocross racing and brands of beer. I look up and see that is what is on the TV, dirt bikes and beer ads. There is no sound, just the cycles spewing mud. He talks almost without stopping, a long stretch of words then his smile popping up regular as road signs. His teeth are the size of baby teeth, wet and sharp, like they belong to some fast little animal. He tells me his name is Tesh, and lets me win two racks of eight-ball.

I go to the bar to order more beer from the girl in the flannel shirt, and look up to see the motorcycles. Instead there is News 11, a blond woman mouthing words. The screen fills with blurry photos of men's faces, and the caption reads, "Wanted for Delinquent Child Support." I wonder if Shelly has thought about giving them my picture, then realize she has probably destroyed them all. I kept one picture of the three of us, smiling in front of a Christmas tree. The camera cut off the tops of our heads. The picture marked my place in the book.

"Can we watch something else?" I ask the girl.

She looks up. "Squeezing the bastards," she says.

For a while I carried the book in the toe of the sleeping bag, but one night I slept out drunk, looking at the pictures, and the next morning it was gone. I'd slept down the beach, away from the boardwalk, and woke up in the dark with the tide inching into my lap. The book was not there. Around me were the tracks in the sand, where somehow the scrapers had missed me. I'd slept through the grind of their engines, their prongs raking the sand.

"What's your story, man?" Tesh asks.

"I could be on TV," I say. "I'm wanted for delinquent child support."

He shakes his head. "Man, that's kids for you." He smiles again with his sharp teeth, pushes his blond hair off his forehead. His flat nose veers off to the left, like a boxer's. I can't imagine that he has any children.

"Where do I cash a check around here?" Tesh asks me.

"Try Dough Rollers Pizza." I've eaten there before, on buffet night.

"Show me where."

"Just down the boardwalk. Can't miss it."

"Show me. I'll buy us a pitcher and a large pepperoni. I need a drinking buddy."

The pocket change is nearly gone. My stomach rumbles and squeezes. Yesterday I left the island; I never wait for them to tell me. Wind off the ocean is cold, full of mist. Here there are no pine trees to break it up. The cold weather makes me think about Billy and Shelly, about where they might be living now, who might be teaching him to ball his fists, to count to ten. Shelly gave me the book on Father's Day when she was seven months pregnant. It had been four months since I left my job at Lincoln Tech, after burning my hand on a braising rod. By then the hand had healed, leaving a thin, pink scar.

The title of the book was *The Extent of Fatherhood,* by Dr. Samuel Beckworth. Shelly sat on the arm of my chair, pulled from my fingers the book I had been reading. "Enough history," she said. The spine of the new book gave a little crack when I pulled open the cover, the pages crisp as new dollar bills. The chapters had titles like "The Mechanics of Nurturing" and "The Emotional Tightwire." I kissed her, patted her stomach, and read the first lines: *Good parenting is often simply a triumph of desire over bad technique. This desire is born of love, and is as old as humankind itself.* The book snapped closed in my hand. I shut my eyes and let a feeling like a sick hangover wash away from me. The words were there, ideas meant to fit inside my head, but these few I'd read jammed me. I was an expert at bad technique; desire died on the couch watching game shows, drinking cheap beer and fingering burn scars. This baby, the rise in Shelly's dress, felt like a test I could either pass or fail, and failing it would prove me to be funneling away instead of—as my father said when he got me drunk—full of lost-dog hope and jerky movements. Every Sunday morning, after I'd tossed the classifieds, Shelly said, "You need to work on your self-image." I told her she sounded like a TV psychologist.

It would be easy to think I forgot about Dr. Beckworth's book, put it in the bottom of a shirt drawer, but I didn't. I dog-eared that book studying the pictures in it—grainy black and whites showing fathers and children together. A man fishing with his daughter, dancing with her standing on his feet, trying on hats in a store. Father and son bowling, reading stories, sleeping in a rocking chair. Everybody was happy. I looked at those pictures every day, pasting together a scrapbook in my head. Ignoring the words was the easy part—I imagined them as being written in some language I couldn't understand, like cave scratchings or Dead Sea scrolls. Shelly would come home from her job where she soldered wires together on an assembly line, and I would be there on the couch, making up pictures of myself with my boy-to-be. In them, I wore cardigan sweaters and neckties and Hushpuppies, we had a nice living room with a stack of *National Geographics* on the coffee table. Then Shelly would find me and we'd argue over my not working. She'd rub her back and not let me do it for her. I would go to a bar and bounce a check to buy more beer. When we were first married, she thought it was cute that our work was so similar; she called soldering "baby welding." I thought about that while I drank the beer. Shelly kept soldering wires right up to the day she went into labor.

Tesh offers me a cigarette from his pack. I take it, then say, "I guess I'm pretty hungry."

"Thirsty too, I bet."

I laugh and blow smoke up toward the TV. I try not to drink on beach nights. It is part of my system of doing things. If they find you drunk asleep on the beach, the police will run you in instead of just running you off. But this is the coldest night in the three months I've lived here. The tin-snap of winter chill hangs in the air, and makes me realize that the summer smells of boardwalk fries and suntan oil are gone. The buoy that marks the entrance to the inlet clangs like someone hammering ice.

Before I direct Tesh to Dough Rollers, I go to check that my things are still stashed beneath the Eskay clock on the boardwalk at Fourteenth Street. I notice a crowd on the beach, a cluster of heads and arms. Boys elbow each other in a circle, moving in the pale evening light. I walk toward them, and they scatter. There is no one else on this section of beach; the lifeguard stands are empty, tipped over on the sand. A ring of footprints marks where the boys have been. In the center of it lies a horseshoe crab.

Some nights I stay up to watch them, dozens of the king crabs pulling out of the tide onto the sand. I don't know where they go, what they are headed for. They move blindly, squarish and helmet-gray, inching forward like small machines. They look like the first things that ever rose up out of the ocean. In daylight, the surf line is littered with shells where the breakers have swept the crabs into the rocks. Their shells are like shards of stoneware. They will cut your feet if you let them. I take the live ones out of the sun, dangle them by their tails and toss them into the water.

This one is not crawling. It is on its back, stuck through with a steel butter knife; its spider legs swipe at the knife. I bend down and see small letters stamped in the steel: STAINLESS U.S.A. Some boy has pocketed the knife from a hotel coffee shop. The crab smells of salt and blood. The legs are rigid as toothpicks; they tick against the metal, the hard shell scratching curves in the sand. I push the knife, and it is solid. While I watch, the black legs stop moving.

Dough Rollers is done up in a merry-go-round theme. All around us, bright plastic horses are frozen in mid-gallop. The pizza warms me and the beers go down easy. Tesh wipes his mouth with a paper napkin, then shoots the napkin into his empty beer mug. He goes to the bar and gives the man some money for a case of beer and a pizza to go.

"Come on and drink with me back at the room," he

says. I begin to worry he is up to something, but then he says, "Come meet the old lady. I'm always dragging home strays." He laughs. I have trouble imagining him with an old lady, the same way I can't see him with kids. He seems comfortable being alone, seems to have already acquired an old man's habit of drinking with strangers in bars. Outside we stand on the boardwalk and the wind slips the seams of my clothes. I say, "Okay."

His old lady is a dark-haired girl of sixteen or seventeen who tells me her name is Tina.

"Tesh and Tina," I say. "That's cute." She laughs and slaps me on the shoulder. I like her right off. She's plain in the face, with muddy brown eyes and thin lips and no makeup. She wears her hair long, and has a hefty bosom that makes her seem chunky somehow. We sit around a folding card table, drinking beer and smoking. The tangle of covers on one of the unmade beds starts to move and shift. I jump, and Tesh and Tina laugh at me. From beneath the covers appears this little girl, about ten, with curly hair so blond it is nearly white. She looks at me with pinkish rabbit eyes and blinks.

"My niece," Tesh says. He bends and plugs in his tape deck, turns up the volume on *Rubber Soul.* It is music I haven't heard in a long time. We listen to "Nowhere Man," and I tell them it is my theme song. Everyone laughs. Tesh tells me his niece is named Becca. She grins and walks over to shake my hand like I've just sold her a car. Tesh gives her a can of beer and she takes a long pull from it, then burps and giggles.

"She's young for beer," I say. Tesh shrugs.

"No, I ain't," Becca says. "I'm an orphan."

"You are not." Tesh taps her on the rump and looks at me. "We're watching her a couple weeks while my brother-in-law and his wife sort out some things." I remember that phrase from the lawyers, and know it means trouble. Paul McCartney is singing; I wonder if I could show Becca how to dance standing on the tops of my shoes. We keep popping beers, pulling off slices of pizza.

The TV in the corner is on and again the sound is turned down. I watch for a couple minutes, expecting news to come on and the blurry faces of the men to reappear, thrown in with motocross racing and beer ads, then gone again. It seems to me that a thing can come back as quickly as it goes away, but on the screen there is only a wrestling match—people wearing masks, slamming each other around. Tesh and Tina watch it and start wrestling in the space between the two beds. They are out of breath and laughing before they sit down again. It makes me happy to see that, the kind of knock-around thing people do when they feel good with one another. Becca is laughing too, from the beer, I think. She gives a high-pitched little girl squeal, like a cheerleader in junior high.

"How old are you?" I ask her.

She sticks out her chin. "I'm thirteen."

"She's eleven," Tesh says. "But she's getting 'em." He tweaks her on the chest, where fleshy bumps slightly raise her T-shirt. Tina slaps his hand. My ears turn hot, and I have the impulse to reach across and hit Tesh in the face.

Tina puts her hands on her hips and throws out her bosom like Mae West, and says, "I guess early bloomers run in the family." Everyone laughs at her joke, and I'm grateful to her for making it.

Becca puts her hands where in a few years her own hips will be, pushes out her chest, and begins prancing around the room wiggling her butt, saying, "early bloomer, early bloomer," over and over in this throaty, piano-top voice. I want to tell her to stay a little girl, not to be in too much of a hurry to grow up and find trouble, to find men and greedy love. Even as I think it she makes herself back into a child, throws out her pale arms and begins twirling, spinning a loopy circle with her head tossed back and eyes closed.

The pizza is gone and the beer half warm. I hear wind shake sand against the storm door and window screens. The music plays while our eyes shift between a dog food commercial on TV and Becca twirling herself into dizziness and giggling. On her feet are these little lacey-top white ankle socks, picking up the grime of the carpet as she spins, turning herself to the point where she has trouble standing, her face shiny happy as she staggers near the beds.

"You're gone to crack your skull," Tina says. Tesh nods his head in agreement. My brain tells me *Get up and catch her before she falls down,* but my legs are too heavy with beer. I tip up a bottle to hide my eyes.

Becca sits on the floor, flushed and sweaty, still giggling. She looks up at me and says, "What's wrong with you?"

It is a question I can't answer. I remember when Shelly asked me the same thing. I sat counting the candy bars inside the vending machine in the waiting area of the emergency room. They sent us there to sit after they carted Billy in for his magnetic scan. The technician told us the big magnet could rip the car keys right out of our pants' pockets. I wanted to keep searching out what came next, so I wouldn't have to go back and think of anything already past. I rubbed at my shoulders, trying to get the feel out of them. All evening I'd sat in a vinyl booth drinking beer and making up scrapbook pictures in my head, then had come home and lifted Billy up on my shoulders, holding his feet in my palms, spinning him around the room. Shelly was shouting, "Stop it, Mitch. He's too young. He's only a baby." But I heard him laughing and laughing, and I closed my eyes so that everything went purple and the spinning felt warm and liquid and made sound come from my mouth. The small heft of Billy on my shoulders felt as good as anything I'd ever known, and I wanted to tell Shelly. She was a shadow in my turning, a voice around me, circling me like a moon. Her sweet perfume was the odor of the dark behind my eyes, the smell of the heft of Billy on my shoulders. She was shouting and I moved inside my eyes when Billy's laughing came through louder, the rounded edges of it broke off into a sound like a tearing of his lungs. I moved and opened my eyes as the room shifted behind Shelly and there was a dull thump like something dropped on wet sand, then Shelly was screaming with her hand over her mouth as I was still gathering the words to tell her how good everything felt, and I ended my turning and saw the swipe of blood on the beige wall above the thermostat. Shelly moved to the phone and dialed.

In the waiting room I watched people put money in the vending machine. Shelly sat beside me; I felt her watching me. A man across the aisle held a bloody T-shirt and a broken yardstick. I had been in this emergency room once before, when I burned my hand. As I sat remembering that, the doctor came out in blue paper clothes and said Billy would be just fine. Shelly cried and shivered and held the doctor's hands. I was happy, but somehow the fact that he would be fine made what I did seem all the more foolish.

When the doctor left, Shelly smoothed the thighs of her jeans and said, "I don't want you around him anymore."

I shook my head. "You think that now," I said, "but it's not what you really want."

"You won't make it as a father. Not till you grow up."

My neck slowly grew stiff, like I'd been in a car accident. I knew right then that if Billy had died from his injuries

Shelly would have thrown her arms around me, that I would have been forgiven and pitied. "I feel older than anybody," I said. An ambulance had pulled up outside, its red lights circling along the walls of the waiting area.

"That's guilt," she said. "It doesn't count for anything. Everything you do is easy." She looked at me like a bored high school teacher explaining some simple problem of geometry. That look was enough to let me know she was done with me, and the sturdiness in her voice after what we'd been through let me see straight down eighteen years, her raising the baby up decent and strong without much in the way of help from me.

Shelly went upstairs in the elevator to stay with Billy overnight. She had her arms around herself. I went home and put my things in the toe of the sleeping bag.

Tesh takes off to find more beer and cigarettes. I stay behind with Tina and Becca. We dance, tossing ourselves around in a loose-boned way that makes me feel good. The tape plays "Michelle," and the three of us clasp hands and turn an awkward, slow circle, stumbling over our feet and laughing. It has been a while since I've held a hand or seen happy females. Becca asks where I live, and I tell her on the beach, in a giant red seashell. The words float up out of the beer I've drunk. She shakes her curls and laughs and calls me silly, so I tell her that big, white dinosaurs come growling every night and wake me up. I tell her animals crawl out of the ocean when the moon is out; I say that in France, people find picture books washed up on the beach. Tina says I sure can tell a story.

"They're not stories," Becca says.

I say to her, "Would you dance with me? I'll be real careful."

Tina is distracted by the TV, pictures of waving flags and fighter jets. I guess the station is signing off with the national anthem. "You don't have to be careful," Tina says over her shoulder, "I trust you."

Becca takes hold of my hands and spreads her feet across my insteps, her white anklets atop my black sneakers. She is as tall as my chest. I balance her arms up and out while we turn a stiff box step, watching our feet. She smells of baby shampoo and sweat. The eyelets on my shoes press into my skin. Tina waves her arms around like an orchestra conductor, laughing, keeping time with our slow dance. When the music quits, I hear sand whisk against the storm door. Becca steps down off my feet. With her weight gone, I feel myself drifting up toward the ceiling.

"I liked that," Becca says.

"Well, good. I liked it, too." I hold out my hand and she gives me five. Tina claps for us, and we bow.

The door opens, smacks open with the wind, and Tesh walks in carrying a grocery sack.

"Road trip!" he says. Another man steps in behind him, young, with short hair and leather biker clothes, a wallet chained to his belt. Tesh reaches in the bag and begins tossing cans of beer to us. The biker goes to the empty pizza box to nibble on bits of crust. He has acne on his pink skin; I want to tell him his clothes are all wrong for his face.

"Where are we going?" Tina asks.

"Up to Assateague," Tesh says. "Spook the ponies. Run the sons of bitches in the headlights."

"What ponies?" Becca says.

"You'll land your ass in jail," I tell him. "Signs say to leave them alone, and rangers patrol all night there. National park."

"Them horses were there before people," the biker kid

says. "Swam up shore off of pirate ships. They won't mind us much."

Becca squeezes my hands. "You go with us."

Instead I say my goodbyes and head for the beach. I tell Becca I have to feed the dinosaurs, that I have to sleep in my seashell and look for story books. I have never really believed that Dr. Beckworth's book might wash back up on shore, but there are times when anything seems possible. During Fourth of July weekend, the tide carried in a bale of marijuana and a survival kit from a Navy life raft.

Outside, wind pulls at my clothes, blows grit into my mouth. My nose runs, and I shiver. By the time I reach Fourteenth Street I'm too cold to sleep, too dizzy with beer. The sky turns from dark to pale gray. I walk on the damp sand above the retreating tide, stepping around beached jellyfish. It is too early for the old people with their metal detectors and dogs. Mine are the only footprints in the washed sand. The tide has brought up rusted cans with the labels worn away, plastic toy soldiers, the broken shells of horseshoe crabs, dirty band-aids and sections of plywood. I walk up three blocks, then back down, my shadow beginning to take shape.

When I look up from the sand, I see Becca. She stands on the boardwalk, waving to me. She walks toward me, breathing white breath, her hair the color of sea oats in the pale light. I push my hands into my armpits and wait for her. The air smells of heavy oil.

"I found you," she says. "It was easy."

"I thought you went off to spook horses."

"I'm scared of horses. When everybody drove off I said I was sleepy."

"You go on off to bed, now. You shouldn't be up all night."

"I want to see the dinosaurs." She stands in one of the raked tracks made by the scrapers.

"You missed them," I tell her.

She frowns. "Then show me the seashell you live in."

I stand and think for a minute, watching yellow foam evaporate on the sand. "Okay," I say. "Follow me." We head back up the beach, stepping through washed up seaweed along the slope of damp sand. I walk the down side, toward the water, and it makes it seem as if she has done two years' worth of growing in the half-hour since I've seen her. As we walk, she takes my hand. I steer her around the jellyfish.

At Fourteenth Street I reach beneath the boardwalk and pull out my red sleeping bag. The rolled up thickness of the bag resembles the whorls on the polished refrigerator magnet seashells in the tourist shops. The only shells I've found on the beach are fragments, scattered pieces. I trace my finger around the spiral of the sleeping bag. "This is where I live," I tell her.

Becca smirks. "That's just a ratty old sleeping bag."

"You have to pretend."

She twists her mouth around. "Pretend is for babies," she says. The wind off the waves lifts her fine hair. She crosses her arms and shivers.

I dig a jacket out of the toe of the bag and snap it around her shoulders like a cape. She looks down at the sand. "Listen," I say, "help me find my book."

"What book?"

"A picture book. The ocean took it away one time, and someday it might wash back up and we'll find it."

She brightens. "Like in France?"

"You got it."

She walks ahead, my red jacket baggy around her. The sunrise looks like a banked fire on the horizon. Miles out, oil tankers float, small as toy boats. I want the sun to come up and warm me, pull people from their houses and hotels onto the sand. Becca steps at the foamy edge of the breakers unfurling on the beach, staying just out of reach of the water. Then she stops and points up the beach. "There it is!" she shouts.

A hundred yards ahead on the sand lies the dark carcass of the horseshoe crab that the boys stabbed with the butter knife. I see the glint of the knife pinning the black shell to the sand as surf washes around it.

"It's a story book!" Becca says, running toward it.

"No," I yell after her. I don't want her to see it, so I run up behind her and grab her under her arms, pinching my oversized jacket in folds. I lift her onto my shoulder, run up the slope and around the dead crab. When we are past it, I set her down again, kneel to catch my breath.

"That isn't a book," I say. "It's something dead."

She rolls her eyes. "I know," she says. Then she turns toward the boardwalk and waves, lifting the jacket. I straighten and see Tesh there, hear him call her in a voice made tiny by the wind.

"I have to go," she says. "We never would've found any book in a million years." As she runs toward Tesh, the empty arms of my jacket trail behind her. At my feet, her own small footprints are pressed in the wet sand, leading away from me, as if she has come up out of the water. Plumes of dry sand kick up behind her as she heads inland. Her tracks there are pegged divots, like hoof marks. Then I can't see them anymore.

The New Us

THE year I turned twelve, my grandfather died and left my father six hundred acres of worthless, scrub-pine property ten miles inland of North Myrtle Beach. "We could go live there," my father said, "if we were rattlesnakes." A month later he received a call from developers who wanted the land for their shopping mall, condos, and golf course ("Those people *are* rattlesnakes," he said). The deal was made by phone, papers were signed through the mail, and within the week we had all this money where there had been so little before. My father and mother called a family conference in the den to explain the significance of what had happened to us.

"How much money?" I asked. I had heard my father tell my mother that he had enough to buy up every vending machine in North Carolina.

"We're filthy rich millionaires," David said. "We're the Rockefellers." David was older than me by four years, which meant, he sometimes explained, that he would always be four years stronger, four years smarter. For a time, I believed him.

"The amount isn't important," my father said. He looked at David and me. "You aren't to tell anyone about this. This is *our* business." He wore the brown Tom's Vending jumpsuit he always had on whether he was making deliveries or not.

"It's far more than we need," my mother said. "I think we should use part of it to help others less fortunate."

My father looked at her and ran his hands through his wiry black hair. "We aren't going to do that, Janice. We're not going to call attention to ourselves."

She smiled. "We could be anonymous," she said.

"We're already anonymous," David said. He looked at me, which was my cue to laugh. I did laugh, and my father glared at us.

The next day my father quit his job with Tom's Vending. He drove his delivery van through neighborhoods where he found children, honking the horn and tossing cases of chocolate cookies to them. Then he parked the emptied truck at the warehouse, and left enough cash to cover the lost food pinned to the clipboard on the steering wheel. At home he grabbed up my mother and danced her around the kitchen singing "The Alley Cat Song." The phone rang and he said, "We don't have to answer that." I stood there clapping my hands and helping him meow at the right places in the song.

That night he took us to Woolworth's, to spend some of the money. My mother, wrapped in her new fox stole, stood in the pet department comparing blue parakeets to green ones. The tiny birds chitted and hopped inside fluorescent-lit cages. My father studied a tank of goldfish. He tapped his finger on the glass.

"You want one of those little birds, it's yours," he said to my mother. "And I mean a cage, food, the works."

"Well, they are cute," she said.

"Done." My father snapped his fingers. He turned to David and me.

"One dollar, each of you," he said. "What'll it be?"

"That's complete bullshit," David said. A clerk glanced up and frowned at us. David pointed at my mother. "You bought her a new fur coat, a new hairdo, a new pearl necklace—"

"Your mother has learned the value of a dollar," my father said. "She doesn't have to be taught the way you two boys do."

David rolled his eyes and thumped the front of an aquarium full of damp half-dollar-size turtles. "There's nothing here for a buck except these shitty turtles."

"Then I guess you get a turtle. Or nothing," my father answered. "And you watch your mouth."

"I've decided against the bird," my mother said.

"Carlton, tell him there's nothing here for a dollar," David said. I looked down at the packet of sea monkeys I held in my hand. The label showed giant cartoon sea animals wearing crowns and jeweled saddles, with golden kings and long-haired princesses mounted on their backs. *Grow Them In Water!* it read. The price was seventy-nine cents.

"David's right," I said. "I mean, Mom got all that stuff." I thought she had never looked prettier. Her auburn hair had been done up in ringlets, and for the past two days she'd worn the pearls. Her skin, she said, made them shine. My father went red in the face, and he whispered.

"One dollar. Take it or leave it."

When we got home, David walked in the door, down the hall to the bathroom without taking off his coat, and flushed his turtle down the toilet. When he came out of the bathroom, my father stood waiting in the hallway.

"Why, David?"

"Just trying to learn the value of a one-dollar turtle," David said. He was taller than my father, his hard shoulders wider.

"David wanted to make a point," my mother said. "But I don't think he should be so ugly about it." My parents were used to the way David acted, as if his behavior were some defect he'd been born with, like a limp or a withered hand. But to me it seemed that during the last few years David had come to hate us for nothing more than being his family. I couldn't understand why. We stood there, cramped in the hallway, until finally David shrugged and looked at me. I stared down at my packet of sea monkeys, at the kings living in the ocean, living in tiny castles.

By the next day the sea monkeys smelled like rotten fish, and I poured them down the sink.

"Son, you don't just throw in the towel that easy," my father said. He brought home books for me on aquatic life and tropical fish. I ignored the books, but my father began spending whole days reading them at the kitchen table. He continued wearing his Tom's Vending jumpsuits, as if reading about fish were his new job. Before long, packages began to arrive by mail: synthetic sea water, protein skimmers, filter systems, submersible heaters. In the den my father set up three large aquariums which bubbled noisily and filled the room with violet light.

Our family no longer spent Saturdays raking leaves or trimming hedges, work David had always despised and I had always loved. Instead my father hired a company called "Lawn Medic," whose workers arrived once a week in a green van, wearing lab coats. David and I watched them mow and trim while we tossed a football in the street. "Let's kill the grass," David said once, "then they'll have to hire Lawn Mortician." I laughed.

Inside, my father would sit on a milk crate, observing his fish. He filled their tanks with plastic diving men and shipwrecks, tiny treasure chests, skulls that blew bubbles. He bought a fourth tank, and before long he and my mother were discussing buying a bigger house ("Who's to say we shouldn't?" my father asked at dinner one night). He began ordering blueprints, which came in the mail with his aquarium supplies. His days were divided between the kitchen table, where he went over house plans, and his milk crate, where he fed and spoke to his fish. My mother circled photographs of walk-in closets and conversation pits in her *House Beautiful*. She signed up for a correspondence course in interior decorating.

One night, David leaned down out of the top bunk, his brown hair swaying. I sat in the lower bunk, reading comic books by the light of a gooseneck lamp. "Here's a prediction," he said. "When we move, we'll go to Irving Park."

"I don't think so," I said. Irving Park was a section of Greensboro we saw only at Christmas time, when we all piled in our Dodge and crept behind lines of other cars to look at the houses decorated for the holidays. The houses ("showplaces," my father always called them) loomed over sloping lawns, guarded by iron fences along narrow tree-shaded streets that circled the golf course. Most of the houses were of white-painted brick, topped with ivy and wide slate roofs, lit up inside with chandeliers we could see from the street. When we drove through at Christmas, security guards stood at each intersection, directing traffic in white gloves.

"That's your problem, little brother. You never think," David said. "We're *rich,* man. We can do whatever we want. Look." He waved a pair of hundred-dollar bills. "A year's worth of allowance."

"Where did you get that?"

"Where do you suppose?" His face turned red with the effort of hanging upside down, the veins in his forearms thickening. He fluttered the bills through the air.

"You don't have to worry about being ugly anymore, Carlton. Help has arrived. Money plus women, and the door to the world flies open."

I watched a sweep of headlights move across the bedroom wall. I shook my head. "I don't get the connection."

"Just wait a couple years," David said. "You will."

"Dad'll kill you if he finds out you stole from him."

He looked at me, his face steadily darkening. "How's he going to know, Carlton?"

I moved my arm in and out of the light from the gooseneck lamp, static sparks snapping off the cotton blanket.

"I guess he won't," I said.

"There, that wasn't so hard, was it?"

"I still don't think we'll move to Irving Park. It's not us."

"This is the new us," David said. "You better get used to it." He smiled and lifted back up into his bunk, where I could no longer see him, just his faint outline pressed between the slats in the thin mattress above me.

* * *

During the next week there was no more talk of new houses. For dinner one night we ate a meal my mother had prepared using her new KitchenMagic Home Workstation. All the food was mashed or chopped into tiny pieces. I couldn't tell what anything was.

David held up his fork. "Can I trade this for a straw?" he said. This time I laughed without being cued.

My father frowned at us. "The food's delicious, Janice," he said.

She blushed. "Well, the machine did all the work."

"I expect that machine will look just fine," my father said, "in your new kitchen." He kept his eyes on his plate, chewing. This offhand method was his way of springing surprises on us.

"New kitchen?" my mother asked. David looked at me across the table and nodded.

"Janice, I talked to a contractor today. We can redo every square foot of this house—add on rooms, finish the basement, new appliances, carpets—for half the cost of buying. We'll be building equity."

My mother smiled. "I never wanted to leave this house anyway," she said.

"When the work is all finished," my father said around his food, "I guess we'll be the only house in the neighborhood with a new swimming pool."

My mother clapped her hands while I jumped up and down and shouted. My father went into the next room to get the sketches the contractor had made.

"Well," my mother said, her face flushed. "I suppose we'll have to learn to swim."

"I can hold my breath underwater in the bathtub," I said. David looked at me and narrowed his eyes.

"Remember this, Carlton," he whispered from his bunk

that night, "if you paint over shit, underneath you still have shit."

For the next month we lived with the noise of power saws and hammers. David and I camped on the den floor in our sleeping bags, watching TV late into the night. When the work was finally completed, it looked as if someone had taken away our old house and left a different one in its place. The outside was covered in yellow aluminum siding. Paper runners guided our steps over thick baby blue carpets. The basement had been redone, with rows of saltwater tanks recessed in the paneled walls. All the rooms smelled of paint and caulking, the plastic wrap covering unfamiliar furniture. Heavy brass deadbolts had been placed on all the doors and windows.

Upstairs, two rooms had been added on: a sewing room for my mother and an extra bedroom for me. The bunk beds were gone; I now had my own furniture, decorated with Washington Redskins curtains and bedclothes.

"You don't even like football," David said to me. His room, our old one, also had new furniture, and a telephone extension on the desk.

"So, boys, not too bad, huh," my father said. "David, it's like you have your own bachelor pad, right?" He grabbed David and squeezed his bicep. This was part of what David had always called my father's "Dad act"—ruffling our hair, squeezing our muscles. Affection had never come naturally to my father, or seemed natural, and there was the strain of longing in his attempts. He had never been athletic, never funny; he'd always possessed a kind of shyness such that it startled me when I'd walk past his bedroom and see him naked from the shower, or when he tried to hug me on birthdays, slapping my back with his open palms. The money allowed my father to indulge his shyness; he no longer had to attend company cookouts, or play on the company softball team. He and my mother quit going out to movies on Friday nights, opting instead to stay in and watch TV movies on their new entertainment center, or dance to records on the new stereo.

David picked up his phone and listened to the dial tone. "Where's all our stuff?" he asked my father.

"Boxed up, in the closet."

Most of our old things—what my mother called her knick-knacks—were gone: the photo cubes on the mantle, my mother's matchbook collection, the King's Dominion poster in the den. Everything was replaced by framed prints and macramé wall hangings.

"Listen," my father said, "we saved a lot of money by not moving, so everybody gets a gift. Anything you like under fifty bucks." He looked at us.

"I'll take the cash," David said. My father frowned and turned to me.

"Me too," I said.

My father frowned again. "That doesn't show much imagination, boys," he said. "But hey, cash it is. Let's go downstairs and I'll give you the grand tour of my new aquarium room."

"We'll catch up in a minute," David said.

When my father left, David pulled me into his bedroom and shut the door. He went to his duffel bag, unrolled a gym sock, reached inside and drew out a roll of hundred-dollar bills.

"Damn, David," I said, "where did you get that?"

He grinned. "From Dad's dresser drawer. A couple bills a night, while he's downstairs doing his Jacques Cousteau act. You should see the stack he keeps in there."

"You're *stealing* it? I thought only those first two."

"Just calm down, Carlton. He'll never miss it. I'm saving for this guy's Camaro. Man, it is one bitch of a car. Four barrel, headers, mags. Give me your fifty bucks and I'll drive you around anytime you want." He smiled. "It's only money."

I ended up giving David my fifty dollars. A week later he rumbled up in the driveway with the battered car, low-slung and bright orange, rattling the windows. He said he'd made a deal for it, and cut his eyes at me. My father ruffled David's hair and went outside with him to kick the tires and peer under the hood. I knew, as I watched them through the front window, that David intended to keep stealing the money, for gas and insurance, I guessed, but somehow it didn't seem so terrible, as if my father's supply of money were a well-spring that could fill itself from below. My father had said that by staying in our house we had built equity. Though I didn't know what the word meant, something about the sound of it gave me comfort. I watched the car spew up a cloud of blue smoke. We're living in equity, I told myself.

At my mother's urging, my father set up an account that paid out regular, anonymous donations to area charities. Our next door neighbor, Mr. Stone, came by at least once a week, and he and my father would stand talking around the swimming pool hole, then come inside for beer and iced coffee. He seemed to be the only friend my father still allowed himself. I sometimes crouched outside the living room and eavesdropped on their conversations, which mostly had to do with investments, mortgages, and home improvements. One time I heard Mr. Stone say to my father, "You'd better watch how you set this thing up, Dade. You'll have the IRS after you."

I didn't have any idea what he was talking about; it sounded to me as if he'd said "iris," which I knew was one of the flowers that my mother had instructed the Lawn Medic men to plant in our new yard. I ran out the door and stood at the edge of the flower bed. I stared at the browned stalks of the plants, trying to figure out which one was the iris, and just how it might be after my father. I knew the idea of it was stupid, and I laughed at myself standing there. But, to be safe, I bent over, pulled up all the plants by the roots, and left them on the curb for trash.

The addition that had been built to accommodate my room stuck off the house into the side yard, next to a large elm tree. When David came in late at night, the downstairs doors and windows would be bolted shut, and he would sneak into the house the same way he'd gotten out: through my window by way of the elm tree. He stayed out till two or three every morning, allowing the Camaro to coast down the last block of our street. Many nights I'd hear his mag wheels scrape the curb, hear him drag himself over the windowsill as I lay beneath the blankets in a kind of half-sleep. Other nights I would wake up and talk to him awhile. He told me I should take notes, that I'd be following him in a few years. One night when I was awake, he came through the window whispering and shushing someone behind him. In the dim light I saw him pull a girl in past my Redskins curtains, saw her long blond hair settle across the rug as she fell into the room. In silhouette her legs were long and thin; she wore tight jeans and a shiny necklace that swung down and tangled with her hair. Her smell—honeysuckle perfume and cigarettes—cut through the dark like a beam of light. She whispered and laughed, and I pretended to sleep, watching her through half-closed eyes.

David paid me to leave my window unlocked. We never discussed any plan for me to do so, but every Saturday when I got up, the ten-dollar bill was on my dresser; I hid them away rolled up inside a gym sock. It would have been payment enough, I thought then, if every night he brought into my room girls with long hair and a honeysuckle smell, girls whispering up out of my dreams. But after that night he never brought another one; they belonged to the larger world I felt looming beyond the walls of our house.

My father decided to build a cave in his basement aquarium room. He hammered out a large opening in the back concrete wall where our dart board had once hung, and together we tunneled out the red dirt from behind it. The hole we made was big enough for my father to stand inside. Around the opening we built a frame of two-by-fours and screenwire, which we planned to cover with plaster and paint. My father promised that when we finished, our cave would look exactly like the caves we'd seen at Hanging Rock Park. "A bear wouldn't know the difference," he said.

He designed the cave to house an oversized aquarium filled with a species of eyeless fish, and other fish, he said, with lights built into their heads. I pictured goldfish wearing tiny coal miner's helmets, like the sea monkeys with their crowns. By this time he was spending entire days in his basement room, feeding and watching the fish, reading about them. He had traded his milk crate for an office chair with casters, so he could roll about the room from tank to tank. The tanks were as big as our console stereo, alive with nurse sharks, lionfish, seahorses, pink coral, and skates. On the carpeted floor moved patterns of light, shadows of the swimming fish. The air in the darkened room churned with the smell of salt, the loud gurgle of aerators. It was like being under the ocean.

He mixed a bucket of plaster, while all around us the fish circled and darted in their tanks. We dipped our hands into the warm plaster and layered it on the screenwire, spreading it around with our fingers. For a long space of time we did not speak, the only sounds those of water bubbling, the slap of wet plaster, and our own steady breathing. David sat behind us on the carpet, smoking a cigarette, flicking ashes into the cuffs of his jeans. The basement was the only place at home he was allowed to smoke, even though my father complained it affected the water quality of his tanks. I watched him blow smoke rings and then stick his finger through them.

"Carlton, how did you spend the fifty dollars I gave you?" my father asked. He didn't look at either of us, but concentrated on his work. With a glance at me David stood and crushed out his cigarette against the bottom of his shoe. We heard his footsteps on the stairs.

"I'm saving it," I said. "For a rainy day."

"Well, that's how a wise man would go about it."

I grabbed a thick handful of plaster and moved around the opposite side of the frame, beside a tank of seahorses. My father followed.

"Carlton," he said. He stopped working and wiped his face on his sleeve. "Son, you wouldn't take money from me, would you?" He looked at me. The plaster felt like wool gloves trapping my hands.

"No sir," I said. "I wouldn't."

"That's what I thought," he said. "But your brother I'm not so sure about." He turned toward the tank of seahorses bobbing in the greenery.

"Hippocampus," he said, reading the plastic label he'd attached to the steel frame of the tank. "You ever noticed how they anchor themselves against the currents? Prehensile tails." He shook his head. "Just amazing."

"I guess it is," I said. He still had his back to me.

"Dad, why don't you just move the money?" I said. "Hide it somewhere he can't find it?" The plaster began to dry on my hands; when I wiggled my fingers it cracked.

"It's not the money," he said. "The money is a symptom, like sneezing when you catch a cold. He has to stop taking it himself," he said. "He has to *want* to stop, or it doesn't mean anything. Do you see that?" I looked at the clipped hair on the back of his neck.

"I guess so," I finally answered. He turned to face me, drawing a deep breath. Then he looked away, and for a minute did not say anything.

"I was thinking," he said, "if those fish live in the dark, it won't matter much to them if they have a cave or not." He laughed, and I let myself laugh with him. I bunched my hands into fists, and all the dried plaster fell away, leaving my fingers and palms bone white.

"This cave is for us," he said. "But what the heck, we'll give them a good home."

We finished my father's cave by covering it with brown and gray house paint. While we worked my mother brought us trays of turkey sandwiches and iced tea. She called us "my two cavemen." When we were done painting, I stepped back, amazed. It looked as if I could walk through the wall of our basement into endless underground caverns, lose myself inside the earth. The aquarium for the cave had been special ordered, with glass an inch thick. My father told me that the fish would live as they were meant to, in water buried in the earth, beyond the reach of light. Within a week the new aquarium—three hundred gallons—bubbled inside the cave. White sand layered the bottom of the tank, the clear water empty of fish. The blind cave fish were to be flown in from the Atlantic Ocean, the electric fish from the Nile River. The exoticness of it all numbed me. I asked my father if I could keep the canceled stamps after the packages arrived.

We stood together, staring at the empty tank, its light on our faces. My father nodded. "Electric fish," he said. "Makes you think, doesn't it?" I thought it sounded like the name of a rock band. Bubbles in the tank rose like jellyfish and broke at the surface.

"Two species surviving in the dark, Carlton. One learns to live without light, without eyes finally. Doesn't need them, right?" He looked at me. "So long, eyes," he said, and I laughed.

"But this other group of characters, petrocephalus bovei, decide they'll just make light, so they can see. Think about that, Carlton. They make light. Like you or me making an omelet."

"Pretty cool," I said.

"It's amazing. They adapt. That's what this whole setup is about."

"What if the kind with the light ends up eating the blind ones because they can't see to get away?"

My father pressed his lips together. "That could happen, I guess, couldn't it?" He looked suddenly defeated.

"Well, it probably won't," I said.
He stared at the empty tank.
"Probably not."

That same week, David bought a hunting bow and set up a practice target at one end of the hole that had been dug for the swimming pool. Cold weather had prevented completion of the pool, and the hole that was left behind ran halfway to the property lines in our backyard, the red dirt piled around it. Gone were the remnants of our old yard, the brick barbecue grown over with vines, the wilted clothesline tangled with tree branches and spider webs, the picnic table covered in lichen, birdhouses rotting away. I could remember times when the four of us had spent our summer evenings in the yard, playing lawn darts, eating fried chicken, my parents sharing sweaty drinks in tall glasses. Somehow, without our noticing, our lives had moved indoors.

On Saturday morning I awoke to the sound of aluminum arrows thumping into the target and clinking into one another. The target was a cardboard cutout of a deer, with a bale of hay set up behind to take the arrows. I watched David through the bare branches of the elm tree. Though it was November and cold, he wore only jeans and sneakers—no shirt. A quiver of arrows hung strapped across his back. All his stolen money was spent this way now—bow and arrows, a new set of barbells, a tennis racket—as if he wanted to be extravagant and didn't know how. I went outside for a closer look.

"Aren't you cold?" I asked him. As I leaned over the edge of the pool, clumps of dirt fell in. David stood at the deep end, pulling arrows from the target.

He grinned at me. "Water's fine, junior. Come on in." I

walked to the shallow end and jumped onto the packed dirt. The red clay gave off a dampness, a fertile, wormy smell. Pale fingers of tree roots grew from the walls. It reminded me of when we'd dug out my father's cave.

David walked toward me offering the bow and an aluminum arrow, which had small dents along the shaft and a wide, razored tip.

"Cool stuff," I told him. "What's it for?"

"Here," he said. I notched the arrow into the string, as he showed me, sighting the deer target at the far end of the pool.

"Keep both eyes open," David said. I sighted and pulled, but lacked the strength to draw the bowstring back more than a few inches. I shrugged and handed it to David. His bicep rose as he drew back steadily and opened his fingers. The arrow pierced the cardboard deer through the leg. He looked at me.

"I'm leaving," he said. He licked the tips of his callused fingers.

"Where are you going?"

"Montana, New Mexico maybe, somewhere out in the wilds." He shrugged. "To not-here," he said.

He drew an arrow from the quiver and sent it into the face of the deer. "You could end up spending your entire life in Greensboro. The money buys our way out." Before I could speak he said, "I know, you're in love with it here." His skin bristled with goose bumps, and his small nipples puckered.

"It doesn't sound like such a great idea," I said.

"What the hell do *you* know about it?"

"I know the only time you ever spent out in the wilds was in a pop-up camper with a refrigerator." He didn't answer, but stood thrumming the bowstring with his fingers.

I imagined him out there trying to find his way to places we'd seen on TV, but ending up lost somewhere on the highway or in the woods. For a moment I felt sorry for him. I started away and he grabbed my arm, pulling me back.

"Listen, don't forget to leave your window open tonight," he told me. His grip relaxed. "I'll float you an extra twenty." This was the first time either of us had mentioned the money he was giving me. I already had nearly two hundred dollars rolled up inside my gym sock, money I would sometimes look at behind my locked door, slowly unrolling each bill.

"I counted last time, Carlton," David said. He scraped dirt from one of his arrow tips. "You know how much money Dad leaves in his sock drawer? Almost nine thousand bucks."

I kicked the dirt at my feet. "He knows you're taking it, David."

He stared at me a moment, then shook his head. "The funny part is, it doesn't even matter anymore. You know what I think? I think Dad would've been happier if he'd kept driving his delivery truck."

"But I don't get it," I said. "Why do you want to leave?"

"You don't have to end up like Dad, Carlton. If you like his damn fish, then go to the Bahamas, dive in the ocean and see the real thing. Get out of the basement."

"You've hardly even looked at his aquariums."

"I don't have to look at them. I live in one."

I rolled my eyes. "You don't even have any place to go, David," I said. "This whole thing is *stupid.*" His face darkened; he reached across his shoulder and snatched an arrow from the quiver.

"Okay, Carlton, here's what it feels like for me every day I live here." Before I could ask what he meant, he notched the arrow onto the bowstring, arched his back and let the arrow fly, straight up. I watched till it flew out of sight.

"It's coming down," he said. I looked up for it, squinting, then covered my head and moved toward the side. David grabbed my arm and held me back.

"Let go of me," I yelled.

"No, don't leave," he said with exaggerated slowness. "I want you to stay here." I looked up again into the white sky and saw nothing. We waited a minute more, but the arrow did not come back. I imagined it flying away, like a bird set loose. I tore my arm from David's grip and made my way to the side of the pool.

"Don't forget your window," he called after me.

Later that day my father's fish were delivered in crates lined with thick plastic bags. There were three each of the electric fish and the eyeless fish, swimming in the clear bags. The dull brown color of the electric fish disappointed me; I had expected them to look like bolts of lightning. The cave fish were pink-white, pale almost to the point of transparency. He placed the bags in the tank to warm, then walked out of the cave and stood beside me, his arms dripping below pushed-up sleeves.

"They're fragile fish," he said. "Sensitive to temperature, pH, salinity, you name it." We stood together, looking into the cave.

"I hope they make it," he said.

"They look okay to me."

"Well, it's too early to tell." He rapped his knuckles on the plaster cave. The fish circled in the bags, above the rocks and coral. "We'll come back tonight and let them try out their new home."

I thought of how far those fish had come to make it here,

to my own basement, and it seemed impossible that the world could be so large. Earlier, I'd found my mother in her new kitchen, just standing, looking around.

"This place is so big now," she said. "When you two are gone it'll seem haunted." I thought of David, his plans for leaving.

"Maybe I won't go," I said.

She smiled. I was taller than her now by an inch or so. I noticed strands of gray in her auburn hair.

"No," she said, "not for a long time."

David and I spent that afternoon in the backyard hole, tossing the football. His strong arm threw hard spirals, centered on my chest. My own throws were loopy and crooked; twice they flew over David's head and toppled his cardboard deer.

"David," I said, "if you leave, are you coming back?"

"Not if," he said. "When."

I shrugged. "Well, are you?"

I watched him, the ease with which he handled the ball. "If I ever need to." I threw a high, arching pass he had to get under to catch.

"You mean if you blow all your money." He drilled a spiral at my breastbone.

"I'm too smart to run out of money."

"When are you going?" I said.

"You'll figure it out," he said. "You'll have your answer soon enough." I nodded, but wondered exactly *how* I would figure it out.

Just then my father appeared at the edge of the hole, against the gray sky. I hadn't seen him outdoors in a while. His face was pale, and the way he blinked made him look startled. I wondered what he had heard of our conversation.

He scratched his head. "We'll have to finish this pool come summer," he said, though I believed the pool would never be finished. He jumped into the hole and lifted his hands for a pass. He caught the ball and handed it to me, and I tossed it to David. We continued in that way, from David, to my father, to me.

"You know, boys," my father said, "that money in there doesn't matter to me. If I lost it tomorrow I'd be just as happy."

David laughed. "You're lying your ass off."

My father set the ball down in the dirt. "You come here," he said to David.

David walked over and stood with his hands on his hips. "What?" he said.

"You don't talk to me that way. Maybe if you'd listen for once you'd learn something."

"What would I learn from you? Maybe 'how to throw away your life on a thousand dollars a day'? You should write a book, Dad."

"Boy," I said, "it sure will be fun to get the pool finished."

"David, if you think money's that important, it will ruin your life."

"You don't know what's important."

"And I suppose you do," my father said.

David shrugged. "I have an idea."

"But showing a little respect to your family, that's not on the list."

I wanted nothing more than for the arrow to fall out of the sky and hit one of us and stop the argument. I wanted to tell David to shut up, to tell my father not to push too hard, tell him that David was leaving. But I knew that my father would not stop him, that David would hate me for telling. Somehow, in my mind, they were the cause of each other.

"Sure it is," David said. "Right behind giving up your life for a bunch of stinking fucking fish."

It happened so quickly that I almost didn't register the fact of my father's open hand swinging up and out, connecting against David's cheek, the sound of it hollow inside the dirt walls of the swimming pool. David raised up his hands, his arm muscles brown and hard. He'd been lifting weights for years now, his body thick and taut. All my father had ever lifted were boxes of snack foods, and they weighed almost nothing. I knew that David could beat the hell out of him if he wanted. Instead he picked up his ball and looked at me, the mark on his cheek red in the cold air.

"There's your answer, Carlton," he said, and walked inside.

"I'm sorry, son," my father said to me.

I nodded, remembering times when David and I were little kids, four and eight, and our father would take us with him on his delivery route for Tom's Vending. We would sit in the back where the boxes were kept, leaning into each other on curves. My father would reach into an open box, pull out a few packages of cookies, and hit them against the steering wheel. "Uh oh, boys," he'd say, "Looks like a few of these got broken. You'll have to eat these, I'm afraid." We'd smile at each other, our teeth black with Oreos. There in the swimming pool hole, I realized how I would like us to spend the money: I wanted my father to buy back his old delivery truck, drive us around in it and feed us cookies. But we were too old to be driven around, and there would be no deliveries to make. Whenever we felt like it, we could abandon the truck, and leave it on the roadside to rust.

* * *

That night I helped my father untie the bags and pull them up and out of the water, releasing the fish. He told me to be careful, that our hands could contaminate the water. For twenty minutes we watched the fish circle the tank, gliding past the rocks and coral.

"Now watch, Carlton," my father said. He reached inside the cave opening and twisted the switch to the ultraviolet light. The tank went dark, and I could no longer see the fish. He bent low, his face to the glass.

"Keep watching," he said, and I bent beside him. We stood, hearing the bubble of the pumps, breathing the salt air, staring into what might have been a tankful of ink.

"Aren't they supposed to light up?" I asked. He pressed his lips together and nodded.

"This is not a good sign," he said. We watched for another ten minutes. When he snapped the tank light back on, one of the cave fish was swimming near the top, upside down.

"Aw, damn it," my father said. He closed his eyes. "I'm killing these fish, Carlton."

The pale fish rolled, its gill flap sucking air above the surface of the water. I wanted to throw up. The other cave fish hovered near the bottom, below the electric fish circling the tank. Within fifteen minutes, another cave fish and one of the electric fish had gone belly up. My father worked frantically, checking and rechecking the temperature, monitoring the salinity and pH, adjusting the flow of air through the pump, consulting his books.

"No, no. Please," he muttered under his breath as he worked. I thought he might cry. I suggested that he just feed them some fish flakes.

He tried to smile at me. "It's more complicated than that,

son," he said. I felt I was in his way, so I went upstairs to my room and sat on the bed. I heard my mother's sewing machine running, David's weight set clanging in the next room. After an hour the sewing machine quit, and I heard other sounds, David talking on the phone, my mother readying for bed, humming to herself. It was quiet awhile, then my door opened and David walked in carrying his backpack. He opened my window and threw out the pack.

"I'm coming back later for the money, when everybody's asleep," he said.

"And then you're leaving."

He nodded. "You could go with me if you wanted. You *should* go."

"I'll see you," I said, and he disappeared out the window into the tree.

A half-hour later my father tapped on my door and leaned in.

"Two electric fish left, that's it," he said. "I've got them stabilized, but they're still in shock. I'll have to watch them overnight." He sounded like a TV doctor discussing a patient.

"A long night," he said. "I could use some help."

"I'm kinda sleepy," I said, and faked a yawn.

"Well, that's okay then," he said. He left, and I heard his footsteps on the stairs, descending into our house. Everything was quiet. I took the money from my gym sock and looked at it. I had lost count of how much I had, and it didn't seem to matter. I thought of adding it to what David planned to take from my father's drawer, the way I had given my fifty dollars for the car, and I knew that with so much money, we wouldn't need to come home for a long time.

I sat in a chair by the window so I wouldn't chance

falling asleep and missing David. For a few minutes I did sleep, my chin on my chest, and awakened myself with a dream of the Camaro coasting noiselessly down our block. I jumped up and threw open the window, leaned out into the dark.

"David," I called in a loud whisper. The winter air cut brittle across my face. My eyes pulsed with the widening of my pupils against the black. There was no light, not even from Mr. Stone's window next door. I listened for the scratch of road beneath the tires of the Camaro, for the scrape of its wheels against the curb. There was only quiet and dark. I drew back inside and closed the window against the cold. Downstairs, my father sat holding a vigil for his fish, urging them to light up, to live in the world he had made for them. Before I left my room to join him, I reached for the window and snapped closed the brass lock.

YAGI-UDA

THE trouble began on a recent Friday evening, when, as a matter of habit, I had arranged myself in the easy chair. Both hearing-aid receivers—the old-style transistor-radio type—sat balanced on my lap, and between them a bowl of shelled walnuts. On the magazine table I placed a bamboo coaster cradling a tumbler of scotch eased down with ice water. I wore electric hunting socks because my feet will chill in winter, no matter how warm the house. Wired up, literally, from head to toe, I pointed the remote control and clicked on WAMR to hear *The Friday Night Big Band Revue,* that week featuring Artie Shaw.

I watched the display on the stereo light up like an airport. I leaned back my head and closed my eyes. Then, instead of music, the speakers burst through with a violent hiss of white noise that startled me so, I spilled my walnuts. The problem, I decided, had to be signal interference from the microwave towers that muck up the fairways across the Naval Academy back nine. When I adjusted the tuner, I found noise across the entire band. With no CDs for the new stereo, no music, no walnuts, no good reason to drink my scotch, I sat there, stuck.

Outside, in the cold, my neighbors' houses shone with strings of colored lights and floodlit cutouts of Santa and his reindeer. I pointed a flashlight at my roof and saw my antenna leaning on its side, blown over by the strong winds blown off the bay. The stuffed owl I had rigged beside the antenna to scare away the seagulls had rolled down against the gutter, its wire feet sticking out. No one bothers with the owls anymore. I remember when every rooftop had one, when boys sold them door-to-door. Now my neighbors' shingles are white spattered with droppings; the rowdy gulls float over their dormers, roost in their chimneys.

After assessing the damage, I went inside and called Janey on the hearing-aid phone she bought me last Christmas.

"Listen, Janey," I told her, "I have to go up and fix the antenna. How about if you and Pete come steady the ladder for me, hold the flashlight."

"Dad, it's nighttime, and there's snow falling. And anyway, *you* do *not* set foot on any ladder. You know you get dizzy."

"Pshaw," I said, a word not part of my ordinary vocabulary, but something I'll say to exasperate her. "I'm not too old to climb my own roof."

"I want you to promise me you won't."

"You're treating me like a child, Janey."

She sighed. "Pete and I will do it, Dad, but not tonight."

The antenna in question is nothing more than a simple yagi-uda modification. Not much on range, but it pulls in the signals of the local stations well enough. I had originally rigged it up for my wife's television. She would watch game shows and shout at the contestants on the screen while she ironed clothes. Sometime after Agnes passed on, I bought my first hi-fi stereo. Pete, Janey, and I climbed to the roof and connected the antenna to the stereo's receiver, then stood and examined the results of our efforts. Not until a few years later did this strike me as strange—standing on the roof with my daughter and the man she would eventually marry, the three of us making small talk like strangers at a cocktail party.

"Raymond, tell me again about this antenna," I remember Pete saying, the wind lifting his hair from his bald spot. "You helped design it or something?"

I repeated the story of my study and work on the yagi-uda, as I'd done for him half a dozen times before, at his request. I knew it was his way of humoring me, of making conversation, getting along. At the time I was still Senior Research Engineer at ENTEC; I retired last August on disability. Janey did not listen to the story. She had heard it enough times before.

"Listen," I said into the phone, "you have no business on ladders yourself."

"Dad, I'm only three months. I'm not even showing." I could hear the blush in her voice at my mention of her pregnancy.

Every Christmas Eve when Janey was a child, Agnes would have me climb to the roof to stomp around in my muddy work boots. "Hurry off to bed!" Agnes would tell Janey, "Santa's here!" After ten minutes I'd stop and sit on the asphalt shingles to smoke a pipe and enjoy the quiet cold. Through the joists and beams I'd feel the bass drum of her running steps: from the den to the bathroom to her bedroom. Remembering all of this, I forgot to speak.

"Dad?"

"I need my music, Janey. There's nothing else I can say on the matter. This is non-negotiable."

"Please don't do anything on the roof. Pete and I will stop by tomorrow."

I treat my deafness as a kind of footrace between debility and technology. As my nerve damage progresses, the world is slowly muted. I even things out with better hearing aids, more powerful stereo equipment. This strategy lets me keep my music—Duke Ellington, Count Basie, Art Tatum—but listening through the earpiece is no better than listening through a tin cup. A matter of poor design. This current stereo was given to me by Janey and Pete just last month, my birthday. Cutting edge hardware, with a remote-controlled multi-disc CD player and a quartz-lock digital FM tuner, but no turntable for my 78s. I admit to this nostalgia, hanging onto those ancient wax sides, stacked away in the basement like some rubber sword I keep to wave in the face of obsolescence. I make no apologies.

The next morning I pulled the ladder from the shed and propped it against the house. The ladder is cracked in places, paint-spattered and held together with duct tape; I won't trouble buying a new one. This past June, I failed to hear the burned-out bearing in the motor of my electric hedge trimmer, and spent the morning shaping my boxwoods until the trimmer smoked and caught fire in my hands. I threw it to the ground, my palms and fingertips seared. Janey and Pete came by the next day and loaded my power tools into the trunk of their Honda. "For your own good," they told me. They hired a boy to come out once a week and care for the lawn. Now she wants me to sell the house—I tell her my clothes, by God, I'm keeping.

During the afternoon the doorbell buzzed, and I expected Janey and Pete. Instead there stood a young woman from down the block—Kate Warner—with her child Mindy in tow. Kate Warner reminds me a bit of Janey—wide, brown eyes and straight hair. Pretty. She smiled and motioned over her shoulder, saying words that sounded like an electric hum to my ears.

"I'm sorry," I said. "I didn't understand." I nudged the volume controls on the receivers in my vest. She leaned toward me, her soap smell pushing into the house.

"Your TV antenna, Mr. Hopkins. It's blown over."

The little girl looked up at me.

"A dead bird's in your rain spout," she said. I leaned down, as much as my back would allow.

"Well, you're mighty observant, aren't you?"

"What's *aservant?*" she asked, and hid behind her mother's leg.

"I'm aware of the antenna," I told Kate Warner. She shrugged, smiled again, and said something else I couldn't hear as she turned away. When she was halfway down the block, I remembered to say thank you. I have the manners of a goat.

Over the years, Agnes became the link in a line of transmittance by which Janey and I could communicate with one another. How else for me to describe it? Evenings, as I sat in my study working on reports, Agnes would tap on the door to let me know Janey needed money for a class trip, a candy sale, or some such thing.

"Why didn't she come to me herself?" I asked without fail. Agnes, God bless her, would shrug; she honestly did not know. I would open my wallet or pull out car keys.

"Tell her to have a good time," I'd say, and transmission of the message was complete. It was that way all our lives together. This was the best we could do. When Agnes died, we lost our link. Pete is a youth counselor for Social Services, and I believe he has been urging Janey to—how would he phrase it?—to try to deal openly with our relationship. Lately, she takes me to dinner so we can reminisce about such things as family vacations. I can recall only brief weekend trips to symposiums where I delivered papers on electromagnetic interference and ate lunches in banquet rooms and officers' clubs. Janey's favorite phrase is this: "We had our own kind of fun."

When Janey was still a baby I would take her with me to the field behind the Navy–Marine Corps Stadium, sit her in the grass while I swung a driver and five-iron, knocking shag balls. Hitting the ball seemed to me nothing but pure motion, a synergy of mind and muscle. I never enjoyed the game of golf—rides in little carts, bets on ten-foot putts. Keep it. An open field I needed, my woods and a five-iron, a shoebox of balls, a tree at which to aim. As I learned power, began to get behind the ball with all my spiraled energy, I found I could send them high over the wall of the empty football stadium, disappearing into its mouth. I felt like Zeus, raining hailstones down on the mountain.

"You see that, Janey," I'd say. She sat, in her clay-stained jumper, looking up at me. Before I realized, she was out of diapers and into dresses, taking off with boys in cars, and I could no longer knock drives over the stadium wall. Now and again I still whiff at balls in the backyard. Short chip shots, pitch and runs. It's a diversion.

Toward dusk, Janey called.

"Dad, we couldn't make it today," she said. "Pete had an emergency at the hospital. Some kid in his Reach Out group tried to kill himself. Swallowed gasoline."

I couldn't think of an appropriate response. "That's very sad," I said, and for a moment felt it. "My antenna is still down."

"None of this could be helped, Dad. You stay off the roof."

"Pshaw," I said.

"I'll be very angry with you." I could picture her as she said this, clicking her nails on the formica, twisting the end of her hair.

That evening I sketched plans for a guy wire system to keep the antenna from falling once it was back up. When I looked out the window, the branches of trees, silhouetted against the streetlights, were shaking in the strong winds. I tried to recall from my sailing days the precise sound of those November gusts ripping off the bay, pushing brine into the streets downtown, right up to the front doors of the shops. I found I could not remember, and so turned on my stereo with the volume up full and for a few moments pretended that the hiss through the speakers equaled the sound of wind, the noise of sailing, the clatter of my past.

By morning, a hard rain fell. I worried that the stuffed owl in the gutter might take on water, though it was made to be waterproof—the feather wings heavily waxed, insides stuffed with dacron, glass eyes cemented in place. In late afternoon, the rain stopped. Outside, a row of seagulls perched along the gutter and on the tines of the downed antenna. The owl looked no more threatening than a lump of wet laundry. When I clapped my hands, the seagulls moved their wings and lifted. I climbed two rungs on the ladder before it began to sink in the wet ground. I stepped down and went into the house. I phoned Janey and got her machine. I've never acclimated myself to this particular technology.

"Janey?" I said, and then waited, as if she might answer. "I don't want to make a pest of myself about this antenna, but I'm not one to put things off." I hesitated. "This is your father," I said, and hung up.

Lately, Janey takes me places on Saturday afternoons—the Naval Academy museum, the City Dock to watch sailboats drift in and out of the bay. One afternoon, as she sat throwing cookie scraps to the mallards, she asked if I remembered a place, other than the stadium field, I used to take her. For a year, when Janey was ten, we lived in Greensboro, North Carolina. On a city playground there lay an old iron radio tower—a hundred feet long, fat as a barrel—mounted on its side atop concrete pedestals. A brass plaque explained it had been the antenna tower for WBIG, during the "golden age" of radio. Kids would dangle from the antenna, climb over and under it, walk its length with their arms held out. Occasionally I would take an hour off work and drive her to the park to see the antenna, to explain its parameters.

Once we went there in the middle of the morning, when Agnes was laid up with the flu. Women in curlers stood talking and smoking in groups while their children played on the swings and seesaws. I sent Janey off to play while I read a journal on—I still remember—terrestrial radio waves. I found an empty bench near a group of mothers with strollers, reading movie star magazines. The secret world of women. When I sat, they stopped talking and looked at me. I straightened my tie and nodded at them; they moved their strollers away. I wanted Janey beside me then, to let those women know she was mine, to legitimize my presence. I put aside the journal and looked up in time to see Janey slip and fall off the top of the antenna and land hard in the dirt below. I ran and drew her up; she held her thigh, skinned beneath the pink hem of her dress. She screamed.

"Shh," I said to her. "You're fine, it's only a scrape."

Her face reddened; she choked on a gulp of air and screamed again. As I held her, the women stared at us. I wished for one of them to come help.

"Please. Quiet, honey," I said to Janey. She kept screaming, and I did not know how to make her stop. I couldn't. The women watched me, shaking their heads and frowning. Sweat ran down under my collar, and I noticed I had somehow misplaced my journal. I lifted Janey and held her in a way I hoped looked paternal to the women, but was meant to muffle her cries against my suitcoat. That was my motive, to shut her up, this injured child. While the women watched, I carried Janey to the car and got her inside, then drove till she had quieted and we could go home.

Now, as we sat on the dock, Janey smiled. "That place was the greatest," she said, as if the incident never occurred, transformed by the alchemy of recollection.

I shook my head. "It's hard for me to remember it," I said. Such lies come easily these days.

Janey called back the next day to tell me that the kid from Pete's youth group had lapsed into a coma.

"I don't understand why this is taking so long," I said, thinking of the Wednesday night jazz show on WAMR.

"The doctors are doing what they can," she said, and I

didn't correct her misunderstanding. Outside, I again went up three steps of the ladder, felt a twinge of dizziness and climbed back down. That night I stood in the driveway wearing my overcoat and hat, watching the stars, trying to remember which of those winking lights are actually satellites in geostationary orbit. I craned my neck and blew white breath at the sky. Minus my hearing aids, I discovered the true sound of night: not crickets chirping or trains rolling past in the distance or anything the poets will give you, but silence, a noiselessness deep as all space.

On Thursday, Janey stopped by to take me out for the day. Pete was at the hospital, talking with the fifteen-year-old, who was slowly finding his way out of the coma. Janey kept herself busy in my presence, fixing sandwiches and tea, wiping the counter, insisting that I eat mustard instead of mayonnaise.

"What would you like to do today, Dad?" she asked, mixing artificial sugar into the iced tea. The new contact lenses she wore made her eyes unnaturally green. I noticed tiny wrinkles around her mouth.

"I'd like to put my antenna back up."

She stopped stirring, and her face darkened. "It's raining today, Dad. And you don't belong on the roof."

"It's my house."

"That boy who works on the lawn, why don't you ask him?" Unconsciously, she rubbed at her stomach.

"He wouldn't know what to do. He'd get it wrong. And I'm asking you."

"We'll get it *fixed,* Dad, but can we not talk about this just now? Let's go have fun."

"You shouldn't feel you have to do that."

"Do what?"

"Insist that we have fun all the time."

She looked at me. "It's probably better if we just don't talk at all."

After lunch, Janey made the decision to drive us to the Armory, where the Ladies' Auxiliary was sponsoring a show, *Christmas Trees of the World*. After we parked, I walked beside her, glancing sideways to notice if she *was* showing yet, if the curve of her stomach was visible through her sweater. Inside, the smell of pine sap mixed with the smell of candle wax and Russian tea.

"So many trees," I said in a whisper, careful in a crowd to avoid the loud speech deaf men are given to.

The trees were decorated with native crafts from their countries of origin: tinwork angels and trumpets from Germany, paper lanterns from China, crystal snowflakes from Ireland, Appalachian corn-husk dolls and beeswax candles representing the United States. People pointed, sniffed the trees, snapped pictures of one another with the trees as backdrop. As we circled the room, Janey smiled and made comments I couldn't hear against the drone of noise.

Most impressive was the tree from Japan, each green-needled branch decorated with a small, white, origami swan, folded from paper that seemed fragile as moth wings. Tiny feats of engineering. Next to us, a Japanese man knelt beside his wife, at the height of his young girl. She wore red barrettes in her dark hair; she was fat, and her black eyes squeezed shut when she smiled. The man gestured toward the tree, talking and laughing, and soon had his girl spinning circles, giggling. Though I couldn't hear, I knew him to be inventing some tale concerning the swan tree, and I felt a sudden stab at never having told such stories to Janey. It seemed in that moment the very business of fathers. I thought of the things I used to show Janey on our Saturday drives—sloping long-wire antennas, planned sites for new office buildings, radio towers I had helped design. Eventually, Agnes would say, "Janey's tired, we should start home."

As I watched, the Japanese man pulled a dollar bill from his wallet, folded a perfect replica of the swans and clipped it to the girl's barrette, which set her off like a wind-up toy, laughing again. I imagined the family at home, assembling their own swan tree. I remembered the aluminum tree we had every year—silver foil reflecting a revolving colored light.

"We should've had a nicer tree," I said to Janey. She stood smiling, watching the little girl, thinking, I knew, of her own baby.

"Did you say something, Dad?" she said.

I shook my head.

"No," I told her. "Nothing."

Last Friday, when I did not hear from Janey, I decided to fix the antenna myself. I carried my wooden tool box balanced on my shoulder. As I climbed the rungs my calves quivered and I had to close my eyes against a slight dizzying. Old age, I thought, is nothing more than an unwitting betrayal of the self. At the top I swung the tool box down against the gutter, braced my hand on the sun-warmed shingles and stepped across to the roof, crouching low to keep from falling backward. Gusts of wind stung my eyes, flattened my trousers against my legs. The asphalt shingles crunched under my shoes as I stepped to the yagi-uda. Several of its elements, the tines, were bent. I straightened them, lifted the antenna back into its brace, then reconnected the receiver wire, which had broken loose. My legs began to feel sturdier on the roof, despite a small ache in my shoulders.

I pulled picture-frame wire and screw-eyes from the tool box to anchor the antenna, which still shook in the wind. When it was fastened down I shook the antenna myself to test its sturdiness, and plucked the new guy wires like banjo strings. It held.

From that vista, I could see to the south the edge of Spa Creek and the tips of sailboat masts. To the east rose the steeple of the Episcopalian church and the white dome of the State House downtown. Two boys kicked a red ball down my street and disappeared around the corner. My antenna, I noticed, is the only one of all the rooftops in the neighborhood; everyone else has cable now, the signals sneaking into their houses from underground, the gray and black of their empty roofs scattered about like playing cards. The cover of clouds overhead made a white cotton batting. The whole, noiseless world stretched empty beneath me—no one raking leaves, walking dogs, jogging.

I walked the pitched slope toward the front of the house to retrieve the stuffed owl from the gutter. The owl threatened to come apart in my hands, the feathers water-ruined and pulling out in clumps, the dacron stuffing squeezing through seams. It smelled of rot. I fingered one of the glass eyes and it popped out, bouncing into the rain gutter. I stood at the edge of the roof, figuring how to wire the owl back together, when a flash of white on the sidewalk caught my attention. The eave of the house obstructed my sight and I leaned out to see. Mindy, Kate Warner's young girl, skipped rope in front of my house, her pink face blowing clouds of breath. She wore a hooded jacket, dull white fuzz circling the hood and cuffs, her shoes shiny in the gray light. As she twirled and hopped the length of rope, her brown bangs jumped beneath the jacket hood and her mouth moved with what I guessed to be the words to some children's jump-rope song. As I walked up to gain a better view, the scuff of my shoes on the shingles made me remember myself as Santa Claus, on the roof, making a racket. Looking at Mindy, I realized that of all those times I had played the part of Santa, I never once saw Janey's face, never witnessed what gladness my heavy steps must have produced in her.

"Hey, you—miss," I said. Mindy stopped and looked around, the rope coiled in a dead loop against the walk.

"Up here," I said, "Mr. Hopkins." Her eyes found me. "I want to show you something. Stay there and don't move."

I walked to the peak of the roof and stood beside the antenna. "I perfected this array," I told her. "It's called a yagi-uda." She looked at me.

"My life's work," I said. Her face gathered in confusion. She tilted her head back and the hood fell away from her dark hair, revealing a red bow and a ponytail. I thought of the Japanese girl at the Christmas tree show.

"Listen," I started over, "how would you like to see this thing full of seagulls?" I patted the yagi-uda. "Picture a big metal tree filled with white birds." For effect, I flapped my arms, slapping them against my sides.

She nodded and laughed, and it seemed so easy, this small joke. I gave the rotten owl a final squeeze and tossed it into the backyard, by the trash bin. When I turned to the front, Mindy had gone back to her jump rope and rhymes. A gust kicked up and I grabbed onto the yagi-uda. The antenna vibrated with the wind, and for a moment I imagined her skip-rope chant being transmitted to me, carried along invisible waves into the tines of the humming antenna, through the bones of my hand, along my arm, and throughout me. Such waves travel in skips and modulations, in swells of resonance. Basic stuff, I thought, first year engineering school. With this thought in my head I lifted a hand to Mindy, turned, and started back down the ladder, that long, shaky climb toward ground.

Spontaneous Combustion

MOST often now, I think of what happened that Saturday only because late at night, when we are in bed talking, my wife will ask me to tell her the story. Twenty years have slipped past since that cold February day in North Carolina, when my grandfather and I had started out to split more oak for the woodstove. My mother stood at the sink cleaning fish I had caught beneath the ice that morning. As a younger boy I had loved to watch her do this job, the way her apron would shine with scales, and how she would twirl around on the linoleum floor and ask if I liked her fancy ball gown. But now I was older and felt embarrassed when she did it.

"Careful, Daddy," she called after us. "Remember your blood pressure."

My grandfather clicked his tongue. "Foolish woman," he said, pulling on his stiffened work gloves. I followed him out to the barn where he lifted the axe from the wall, and the two of us tromped out into the yard. The ground lay quilted with a crunchy snow, and I could smell suet we had hung out for the finches.

"Now, look here, boy," my grandfather said. "There is no such thing as what the common man calls accident. You might remember how that child murderer, Saul, on his journey to Damascus, was struck blind and fell prostrate in the road. Now, that was no accident, but was the working of the Lord. Saul was made blind that he might see."

A white breath, like steam, blew out of his mouth. He grabbed the head of the axe, held it at arm's length, and turned full circle, like the weather vane on top of the barn.

"Always keep such a circle," he said, "that way there'll be no mishap."

He steadied a log and spit into his gloves. On the first swing the axe rang a glancing blow off the side of the log and bit cleanly into the middle of his instep and halfway through his foot. I remember it looked so much like a Saturday morning cartoon that I almost started laughing. My grandfather sucked air through his teeth and his face turned white as the patches of snow on the ground. A coppery red pool darkened the snow beneath his foot.

"It's bad, son," he said. "Run in and tell your mother to call the hospital."

A strange quiet enclosed us while we waited for the ambulance to arrive. I remember my mother leaning at the porch railing, looking down the street, the knife still gripped in her hand. The paramedics arrived and began attending to my grandfather's foot while I explored the blinking, squawking machinery in the back of the ambulance. My hands were shaking, but more from excitement than fear. I was fourteen then, and such a gory accident seemed exhilarating. Finally, the ambulance drove off howling with my grandfather inside. My mother and Aunt Cleo piled into the Dodge to follow.

"Daryll, now you watch out for yourself while we're gone," my mother called through the car window. "Watch that fire in the stove. Answer the phone for us. You're old enough to take care of everything." Her face was red from crying and it made me want to take care of things, to take care of her. At that point in my life, I felt I could.

It was two weeks before my grandfather came home from the hospital. That evening, in the middle of watching "Jeopardy," he removed the sock and bandage so I could see where the doctors had amputated. His foot looked like a knot on the end of a tree branch. The skin around the wound had browned and withered, like the skin of the mummy we'd seen on our field trip to the Natural Museum.

"I spent six months in a foxhole during the war," he said. "Never had so much as a nosebleed. And here I disable myself just trying to keep the house warm."

Later that night, against doctor's orders, he limped out to the barn to begin what he called his new project. After two hours, he had not returned, and my mother sent me to look for him. I found him at the workbench with his shoe clamped in the vise, a hacksaw in his hand. He cut through the leather so the toe of his shoe fell into the dirt. Then he showed me a small box he'd fashioned from sheet metal, its sides neatly folded and soldered along the seams. He held it in his hand like a cup. On the closed end of the box, several layers of tin had been stacked up and riveted together. He placed the metal cup where the toe of the shoe had been. A perfect fit.

"Look at that. Better than any you might buy," he said. "The Lord guided my hand." I nodded, though thinking that the Lord probably had no particular interest in semi-skilled labor.

He riveted the metal to the leather and slid the shoe over his bandaged foot. He stamped his foot twice on the floor and kicked the lawn mower.

"If only the rest of me felt this good," he said. His voice sounded heavy. I looked up at him and he nearly smiled.

After that, things settled down for a while. My grand-father clomped around the house in his new shoe and even picked up his trumpet again. We heard him at night when we were downstairs watching television. He would be up in his room playing "A Mighty Fortress Is Our God" and the opening notes of "Nearer My God To Thee." Every evening after supper he walked out into the yard with his red, white, and blue basketball to take his customary two hundred foul shots, a practice he followed with his typical religiousness. He stood on a patch of worn-down lawn and threw the ball at an old plastic laundry basket nailed to a tree, the bottom cut out of the basket. He'd never played basketball and took his nightly dose of foul shooting as he took his morning dose of cod liver oil and brewer's yeast—it was tonic, approved by his doctor. One evening, I kept a tally (which he never would), and watched him sink one hundred and ninety-five out of his two hundred shots. I told him about it, and he shrugged.

* * *

On cold Saturdays when the air was brittle, I would head out to the junior high field with Drew Griffin and Wallace Harper to practice football. One Saturday, my grandfather came out to the field. I saw him walking over the top of the hill, his right leg as stiff as a cane.

"What's your grandfather coming out here for?" Wallace asked.

"I don't know," I said. "Maybe I forgot to do something."

He hobbled up to us, out of breath, his face white as ice. The three of us stared at him. He drew a deep breath and spoke.

"The Lord in all His infinite wisdom has provided us with various forms of work and disport that we might strengthen our bodies to His great glory."

I looked at the stunned faces of Drew and Wallace. They weren't used to hearing anyone speak that way except in church. My grandfather looked down and spoke quietly to Wallace.

"Son, hand me the ball and go long."

Wallace pitched him the football and took off toward the goal posts while Drew looked on as though he were watching the end of the world. I admit I was just as surprised. Although I knew my grandfather to be able and strong, it was rare that I'd seen him have any fun, take any enjoyment from things. It was as if it weren't fitting for the former pastor of the Yanceyville Wesleyan Assembly to seem frivolous. The narrow path was also austere.

My grandfather cocked his arm and leaned on his back foot as if he had played all his life. He motioned with his hand, pushing Wallace further down the field, and Wallace shouted "I'm open!" as my grandfather stepped and flung the ball. It wobbled in the air like a goose with a shotgun wound and dropped, twenty yards short. The look of disappointment on Drew's face was profound. I felt my own face burn.

My grandfather clicked his tongue.

"Well now," he said. "Let's infer that throwing just isn't my game. The Lord gives us talents in some areas and denies us in others."

"That's okay, Mr. Jackson," Drew said, speaking too loud. "It started out like a good throw."

My grandfather held up his hand. "What I mean is I have faith that providence has supplied me the means for kicking the ball. I think I'd like to have a go at that."

"I don't think you should, Granddad," I said. "I mean what with your bad foot and all."

"I'll be fine," he said, and nodded. "You'll hold the ball for me."

We were a good forty yards from the goalposts. Wallace carried the ball up and bent to snap it to me. I got down on one knee while my grandfather backed away. I yelled "Hike!" and the ball popped into my hands. I put it point down on the ground and spun the laces toward the goal, the way the pros did it, pressing the tip with my finger. My grandfather trotted up limping and swinging his arms, the coins in his pants pocket jingling. Then he planted his left foot and swung hard with his right. I watched it close and saw the flattened metal tip of his shoe meet the brown leather as square and solid as a hammer hitting a nail. A shock, like electricity, passed through my finger as the ball hissed away from me. I turned to watch it tumble, perfectly, end over end, and split the goalposts like a missile, still climbing. He clapped his hands together and laughed a ringing, wheezing laugh. Wallace took off to look for his ball and Drew stood shaking his head. I laughed too, and at that moment I would have happily sacrificed half my foot to be able to kick a ball beyond seeing.

Every year, on the first Sunday in March, the three of us, my mother, my aunt, and I, piled into the Dodge to visit the graves of my father and grandmother. It was always the first Sunday in March because my parents had been married then. My mother would slip quietly into the cold light of my room and shake my foot to wake me. We had to leave before dawn to be back in time for church. I would rise, thick with sleep, to the edge of my bed, and pull on my pants and shirt and boots. My mother took with us the thermos of coffee and a brown bag filled with sausage biscuits wrapped in wax paper. My grandfather never went, though we would find him sitting stiffly on the edge of the couch, dressed for church, when we got home. It always seemed strange to me that he would not visit the grave of his own wife, but the weight to the silence of those gray mornings prevented me from asking why.

The cemetery lay bare in winter, minus the gaudy field of pastel plastic flowers we would find there at Easter. As always, my mother brought a potted azalea for her mother's grave, and I staked it to the frozen earth with bent pieces of coat hanger. My aunt brought Windex and a sponge to clean the headstone. The two of them stood, holding hands, and I heard their breathing and the sound of tee shots from golfers at the driving range next door.

"I just realized, I was your age when she died," my mother said. "Your grandfather never got over it."

I looked up at her, but she had moved off toward my father's grave. Aunt Cleo laid a firm hand on my shoulder.

"Let her be," she said. "She needs to be alone with him."

Then my mother stepped up to my father's grave and spent a long time reading the few words written on the black marble. She never brought flowers, but instead would suddenly and quietly drop her scarf or her hair ribbon or even a button torn from her blouse. She always seemed embarrassed by these gestures, as if we'd witnessed some kind of intimacy, which, I suppose, we had. Only once, several years later, did I see her cry, on what would have been their twentieth anniversary. Her bright tears fell, silent as snow. I could nearly taste her tears on my tongue. I was home from college then, and had missed this ritual for the past two years, nearly forgetting it. I went to her and put my arm around her waist and held tight. She lifted her arms to me. I gave her my handkerchief and she smiled and wiped her eyes. Then she left it sitting there, a small, white square atop the slab of black marble.

After the accident, all the wood-chopping chores fell to me. This was during the oil crisis of the early seventies, and we had shut off the furnace and tried for that winter to stay warm using only the woodstove. There was much work in it. My grandfather avoided the woodpile as if it were ground cursed by the devil. So, I was surprised the Saturday morning he followed me out to the woodpile and sat on the rotting picnic bench to watch me. Between his feet was his red, white, and blue basketball, and he was still winded from that morning's foul shooting. He watched me haul unsplit logs from the back of the lot, rubbing the big rust-brown spots on the backs of his hands. He picked up a stick, drew out his knife, and whittled the stick to a point. He used it to tap out church songs on the metal tip of his shoe. I looked at him every few minutes and smiled, and he nodded at me, not speaking. I propped a log up on the other stump and brought the axe cleanly down through it. It gave a satisfying dry crack, exposing the white wood inside. I could smell the sweet oak. I brought the axe down again and again, stacking the logs behind me. Finally my grandfather spoke.

"Son, I followed you out today because you have come of a certain age and I believe it's important for you to understand some of the many uses that the Lord has found for fire."

I buried my axe in the stump and wiped my face, wondering if he meant this as some old-time-religion version of sex education. He continued.

"Now, I know you possess in your mind a certain *a priori* knowledge about this most frightening of God's creations, leastwise you wouldn't have reason to be cutting up those logs for the woodstove. But there are ways in which the Lord employs fire that in your youth you may not see nor immediately understand. Like when God used a burning bush to call Moses. That bush burned with the fire of God and was not consumed." He stopped and wiped his mouth with his finger.

"There is a different fire that burns in the soul of a man. It is a fire that leads many down the wide path of temptation and sin. It is a fire that is a source of longing and hardship. It is a dark fire, a blood fire, a burning, dangerous thing."

His voice rose to pulpit level as he spoke, and his eyes focused over my head. It was hard to look at him.

"Son, this fire that I've been going on about is the fire of love. Now, I don't mean the redeeming love of our Lord, not *agape* love, but the earthly love between man and woman, *eros*. For a woman, love is necessary for the nurturing of children. But inside a man it's a place of danger, like standing at the edge of a cliff. I know because once I stood at that cliff and fell into that fire. The Lord in His mercy spared me that I might tell others, and I am here today to warn you."

I could hear Wallace and Drew on the next block shouting to each other for the football. I wanted to be with them and not here, trying to figure out what he meant.

"Certain episodes come into play, by which the Lord sends us warnings," he continued. "There was a man who lived over in Randleman when I was a boy. Odus Jamerson was his name, though I never met him. But he was famous in these parts after what happened to him. Now, Odus Jamerson was not one who was mindful of women, who burned with *eros*. He lived fifty-three years, gratified with nothing but forty acres of soybean, a chicken house, his Indian arrowhead collection, and three decent dogs. One Sunday, though, he went to a church picnic and met up with Sarah Reynolds, who was Jim Martin's cousin."

He stopped his story long enough to brush away a wood beetle crawling along his pant leg.

"Not many days passed before Odus took to Sarah and before anyone knew what had happened, he'd thrown the dogs out and gotten himself married. They weren't together two weeks before this so-called accident happened. The way it was told is that one day Odus Jamerson sat in his easy chair loading up his shotgun for squirrel. Sarah was out in the kitchen making candles when she heard this awful whoosh and then a noise like all the thunder in creation. She rushed out and found a thick hanging of smoke and a two-foot hole in the wall. What happened was Odus Jamerson just went up in flame. The fire came from *inside,* within him, and burnt him right through to ash. It didn't singe so much as one thread of his clothes, they were laid out in the chair right where he'd been sitting. But there were ashes down his shirt sleeves and pant legs and inside his boots. The police doctor called it spontaneous combustion. A rare thing indeed. Nothing but ash. The heat from the burning set off those shotgun shells and blew the hole in the wall. Now, in the years since, I have come to know it as portent. A sign from the Lord about the destructiveness of fire, of love, about staying away from the edge of that cliff lest we fall."

He stopped and lowered his head, his mouth still working with small movements. The sounds from the football game were gone, and there was only silence around us. My face burned, as though heated by the image of that burning body. And his face, when I looked up at him, was distorted, the way a tin roof buckles in the sun. There was spittle on his lips, and his eyes were small and shiny like hen's eyes. I thought to ask him then about my grandmother—felt my first anger that he avoided her memory—but wasn't able even to look at him. I looked instead at the brown handle of the axe, and down, at the sharp angle made where the axe had cleaved the tree stump. An amber drop of sap rose in the cut, and it reminded me of watching my grandfather cut off his foot and the swirl of blood beneath it, and I knew it would be hard for me to lift the axe again without feeling something like fear.

I wanted to say many things to him then. I wanted to tell him how nice it was at the graveyard on those March Sundays, not too cold or sad, how good it sounded when a club struck a golf ball. But as I thought of what to say, something like a well opened inside me and all my words fell into it. So I stood there and said nothing. Finally my grandfather raised himself, gathered his basketball, and limped back to the house.

* * *

That night I lay in bed, my muscles sore from splitting wood. As I slept, I dreamt of my grandfather. He was Odus Jamerson, sitting in an easy chair loading shells into a gun. Only the shells were footballs; big, full-sized footballs that somehow fit down the barrel of the gun. Then I looked into his face and heard a whoosh and he was clothed in flame, in a fire that left him not burnt but frozen. His body was frozen solid inside his clothes and the shotgun between his knees had formed tracings of frost on the barrel. There was frost in his hair and on his eyelashes. Then his fingers and ears and cheeks began to fall off him in chunks, like ice broken from tree branches. The police doctor came in and used an ice axe to break him apart, then lifted the pieces with tongs and dropped them into a bag. I woke up shouting and my mother came in to find me. Her soft, cool hand on my forehead brought me back to sleep, and I remembered that soothing touch in my dreams.

The next morning I awoke to a brightness that filled my room as if the walls had been painted with light. I knew right away there was new snow on the ground outside. I ran to the window, lifted the shade, and watched the big flakes toss in the wind like dandelion seeds. I walked out to the kitchen, where my grandfather sat propped in a chair before the woodstove. He faced the window, light shimmering on the nickel-white fringes of his hair. His shoes sat on the woodstove drying and hissing, and he had the army blanket pulled high around his neck. A fresh stack of logs leaned beside the stove, and snow from them had melted and puddled on the floor. I went to the stove and lifted his half-shoe. It was warm and wet and heavy.

"I'm cold," my grandfather said. I noticed his bare feet against the linoleum floor.

"Granddad, it's your feet. You should wear these."

"No, I don't believe so," he said, and looked away. I set the shoe back on the stove and stepped over to him, then lifted a corner of the green blanket and carefully tucked it around and beneath his feet. He smiled, his lips thin and cracked.

"Better," he said. "Thank you."

There are times now on Sunday afternoons when I am dozing in the recliner and my wife rouses me from it and sends me to the yard for more firewood. When days are cold enough to be bitter and the gray sky smells heavy with wood smoke, I can close my eyes and imagine him there with me as I gather the logs. He is always the same in my daydreams, sitting on a rotted picnic bench, holding his basketball beneath his arm, rubbing the spots on his hands, tapping out hymns against the toe of his shoe. On those days I wish he were here again so I could tell him some things. I would like to tell him he kicked one hell of a football. Or I might remind him of how perfectly that ball flew, and the look on Drew's face, and maybe that would make him laugh again as he did then. I would like to see that. But above all I would tell him the most important thing I have learned in the eighteen years since he died. That it is not fire we should fear but rather the desolate coldness of being alone. For it is that which robs us of life.

Just last week, watching football, I fell asleep on the couch in front of the fire with my stocking feet propped on the hearth. I awakened with a searing pain in the soles of my feet and I jumped up yelling, convinced for a moment in my half-awake dream that I was Odus Jamerson, consumed in my sleep by a fire from within. I hopped from foot to foot and tore off my wool socks, half expecting to find them full of gray ash. Then I noticed my wife, who sat on the couch, convulsed with laughter. Her laugh was high and clear and full of love for me. I smiled at her and realized anew that if I am to be consumed by anything, it will be my love for her. We huddled together beneath the quilt and I put my warm feet on her legs. She was still laughing and I pulled her close and kissed her, grateful for warmth in winter.

Smoke

BOTH envelopes dropped through the mail slot the same afternoon, just a day after I'd gone back to court to pay off an eighty-dollar fine I'd earned for collaring my ex-wife's lawyer in the men's room on the first day of our divorce hearing. I sat at the folding card table in my kitchen and opened the final notarized decree that made legal my broken-up marriage with Debbie. I took that paper and stuck it to the wall with a Bic pen stabbed in the sheetrock. During that time two years ago I was full of such acts, pretending for no one's sake but my own that I could be a hard-ass, that none of it bothered me.

So here's where I stood: I was thirty-five years old, coming off eight years of a marriage springing leaks I ignored until the whole thing was sinking, and as many years teaching geometry and woodshop to tenth-graders. I was done with school, didn't care if the children could calculate isosceles triangles or build bookends, and so had made plans to abandon Winston-Salem, head south to Florida, and find a job wiring houses in the aftermath of Hurricane Andrew. In my heart this passed for a romantic gesture, which according to Debbie I lacked in abundance. I'll show her, I thought, but really thought of a job that wouldn't put me on disability if I could keep myself insulated and grounded. With that same Bic pen, I'd written on the wall, *How much will bring her back?* and beneath it kept a running tab of what I thought I could earn and what I might swing in the way of a house or a new car. I'd planned to just buy my way back into our old life.

The second envelope contained a quick note scrawled in pencil on a scrap of yellow paper, from Purvis Hoyt, my Uncle Eck's roommate of seventeen years:

> Your Uncle Eck has forgiven his cigarettes, Robert. This is not good, and I trust you'll expedite a visit. Consummation begins when a man starts shelving old debts.
>
> —PH

I had planned to visit the two of them before I left for Florida. Eck especially, as we hadn't seen each other since my marriage began to crumble. Years before, on the day of my graduation from Konnoak Elementary School, my father tossed his clothes and golf clubs into the trunk of his Buick and left us, and a week later Eck moved in to help with the bills and keep the hedges trimmed. He practiced his fatherliness toward me like he was learning it through a correspondence course. He taught me to rebuild lawn mower engines and fishing reels, to smoke cigarettes the right way, to hold doors open for ladies. Evenings, we stayed in the basement of our house, playing poker. He filled those penny games with grand drama, calling himself Abdula the Turk, and me The Professor, for the tortoise-shell glasses I wore. I knew little about him that first year—other than he was my mother's brother and he'd given up a job as a motorcycle cop to work in a factory—but growing to love him was easy enough that I didn't have to think about it. He stayed with us until the year I started high school.

I read Purvis's note again, and still it made no sense. I studied the neat ellipses of his handwriting. My Aunt Lily liked to call him a worn-out fop, and there was some truth to that, but I knew him, knew he wouldn't lie to me where Eck was concerned. Before I went to see them, I picked up the phone and called Debbie.

"You again," she said.

"I'm thinking of leaving," I said. "Florida."

"Last week it was Montana."

"But I'm serious this time. I think I might really go."

"That's probably healthy for both of us," she said.

"Especially for me. I hear the air is nice and clean down there." Without meaning to, I put an edge on my words.

"You're angry again."

"Not again. Still."

"Drop me a postcard," she said.

"You could go with me, the two of us. Think about it for a minute." She did, and then hung up.

Eck and Purvis lived in a cramped apartment at the Robert E. Lee Hotel, a room with browned window shades and a rusty sink, bars on the windows. The tables and shelves were covered with beanbag ashtrays, tiny globe banks, novelty soda bottles, and joke cigarette dispensers—dusty souvenirs that Purvis had collected during his years of traveling around wholesaling cardboard boxes. Old photographs were thumbtacked to the wall: Eck in his police uniform, standing in a snowstorm on the White House lawn, Purvis dressed for Halloween as Lawrence of Arabia. They'd been friends since the day Eck helped Purvis push his Dodge Dart out of a ditch.

"You come bearing your shield, Robert," Purvis said as he let me in the door. "All debts paid, no shame in that."

The smell of their apartment—cat food and boiled peanuts—erased the six months since my last visit. Eck's ten-speed racing bike hung by its frame from coat hanger hooks looped over the curtain rod. Along the stained walls of the room leaned the knee-high stacks of books and magazines that Purvis collected—*The Iliad, Popular Science, How To Win Friends and Influence People.*

"You're losing your hair," Purvis said.

I laughed and ran my hand over my scalp. "My hair, my wife." I wanted to be seen as the type who could joke about his troubles.

For his part Purvis looked the same, deep sun wrinkles and thick, white hair, eyes pale blue and bloodshot. He sported a tiny bow tie, and had about him the smell of cologne samples from magazines. He still wore the Empire State Building cufflinks on his yellowed shirt cuffs. I remembered when I would visit as a teenager, and he'd wink and point to one of the tiny windows, the fifty-fourth floor, where he said he once met Betty Grable on the elevator.

"Sorry to hear of your problems," Purvis said.

"Where's Eck?" I said. "What's this about forgiving cigarettes?"

"Robert, I'll ask you to sit down." He took my elbow and led me to Eck's army cot.

In the bedroom where Purvis slept, I heard Desdemona scrape against the door. Desdemona was Purvis's pet goat, which he'd ordered out of a catalog. Purvis fed her cat food and beef jerky, the sugar cake he bought at Dewey's Bakery. She was an oddball breed, a fainting goat. Startle her and she'd go down, her pink eyes shut tight. I took off my shoe and flung it against the wall and sure enough heard Desdemona slump to the floor on the other side.

"They've sequestered Eck in the hospital," Purvis said. "His lungs."

"What the hell are you talking about, Purvis?"

"Cancer. Black spot on the X-ray, black spot on your existence. Old story."

Eck had smoked Camels since his days in Washington, where he had worked guarding President Roosevelt. During our basement poker games he taught me three rules for smoking: inhale deep, keep the tip dry, buy a new pack before the old one gives out. I remembered he would hold his pack of Camels up to the bathroom mirror to show me his favorite trick, how one of the words printed on the side, CHOICE, would not reverse itself in its reflection.

I put my shoe back on and paced around the room.

"How come nobody told me about this?" I said.

"Well, now, some might attribute that to kindness, not adding to your already substantial troubles."

"Damn it, Purvis—"

He held up his hand. "Not my place. And his sisters would have skinned me."

"So what are you telling me?" I tried to keep my voice steady. "Eck's going to die?"

Purvis pulled at the edges of his silver hair. "That's what

he maintains. God help us, this family is genetically wired for pessimism."

"I have to see him. He's in Baptist?"

Purvis picked up a donkey cigarette dispenser and studied its mechanism.

"What we have to do," he said, "is take him out of there. Duty, loyalty. Call it whatever you like." He opened the door to let Desdemona out of the bedroom. She was smaller than I remembered, her yellowish coat neatly brushed. She came and lay across Purvis's feet.

"What are you saying, Purvis? We can't just take him out. He's sick, for godsakes."

Purvis nodded. "It's your decision. You go see him, Robert. Then decide."

When I got there, the sisters—my aunts—had him surrounded. Eck looked thin in his bed, but this didn't bother me much; he'd always been thin. What he'd lost was the wiriness that put a rubberband snap in even his smallest movements—drinking coffee, shifting gears. Lily and Ava and Cedelle were all there, looped like beads around the foot of the crank bed. My mother had been the youngest of them and had died first, five years earlier. Eck had an oxygen tube taped to his nose. With the bed set at half-tilt, he looked as if he'd caved in, buried at the bottom of all his sisters. They were talking of him, about him; no one spoke to him, and I worried he might be unconscious instead of just asleep. He stirred a little when I touched his foot through the blanket.

All conversation had ceased the moment I walked through the door, and then my aunts started in on me, saying how they missed my mother, how I looked older, as if I'd been away to junior college instead of living in exile from my old life. No one mentioned my divorce from Debbie or the rumors they must have heard, the months of late night phone calls, squealing tires, slammed doors. The noisiness of love unraveling.

They gave me hugs and patted my back, their charm bracelets jingling, hairdos stiff with spray. I had a ten-year-old's urge to wipe away their kisses. They picked up where they had left off, discussing Eck's assertion that he had slipped and fallen on the bathroom floor that morning. Tea-time chitchat, everyone talking, no one listening. Cedelle suggested that the pain drugs were doing things to Eck's mind, that he had dreamed the whole thing.

"Like *hell* I did," Eck said, his voice full of wheezing. He rose up on his elbows and saw me standing at the foot of his bed.

"Hey, look who's here," he said. "The family criminal. You beat up a lawyer, they ought to give you a medal."

I laughed and hugged him, his grip on my shoulders still strong. "I didn't exactly beat him up," I said. His smell was a mix of ammonia and the lavender tonic he used to slick his hair.

"But not bad for a math teacher," he said. "Tell me, Robert, what's the capital of Siam?"

I grinned and shook my head, remembering the joke as an old leftover from his time at our house. A moment later, slower than he had been, Eck whispered "Bangkok" and tried to goose me in the groin. When I blocked his arm with mine I saw him wince, a quick suck of air through his teeth. Lily told me to stop riling him up.

"You're not feeling so well," I said.

"Black coffee and a ten-miler would do me."

"The coffee I can handle," I said.

He nodded. "Always my favorite nephew."

I found the vending machine in the snack bar downstairs.

The coffee poured out into a paper cup with a hand of five-card draw poker printed on the side, a pair of tens, queen high. Without any thought, I knew how I'd play it—go safe, fold early, lowball somebody with some minor-league bluffing. Eck hated the timid way I played.

When I stepped into the room with the steaming cup, Lily grabbed it away from me and poured it down the sink. She spoke in a harsh whisper, mentioning diuretics, stomach acid, and free radicals (for a minute I thought she meant me). She asked if I were trying to kill him. I looked at Eck, deep asleep again and snoring. It seemed impossible then that anything, cancer or not, would be enough to end him.

Instead of the coffee, Lily opened a can of something called NutriSoy, which came with a little straw and a picture of a nursing mother on the label. She set it among the tissues and bedpans on the night table. For when he woke up, she said. The sisters started talking about various dead members of the family and how Eck looked so handsome in the dark suit he'd worn for his retirement. I thought of Purvis with his goat asleep on his feet, of my plans for leaving Winston. I thought of the day Debbie asked me to move out of our house, how final it all was for her, how she wouldn't look at me the next day while I packed the car, and how I packed it trying to think back to some exact moment when things had gone wrong. Of course, there was no such moment; things go bad a little at a time. She stood in the doorway with her robe pulled tight around her, and I regretted that I hadn't had one last look at her beneath the robe, that when we last slept together I hadn't known it was the last. There in Eck's room I felt the same pull I'd felt leaving our house that first time, like gravity along my spine. I felt as if some unnamed thing had been taken from me, and I craved it like water. I took a breath then, and decided Purvis was right, we had to get Eck out of there.

Eck's bicycling shorts, racing jersey, and shoes were small enough to fit in the pockets of Purvis's old-man slacks. The next day we walked into the hospital in the bright sunshine of a Saturday afternoon, and Purvis tossed the clothes across Eck's bed. He looked at them, managed a weak smile, and without a word sat up and pulled the oxygen tube from his nose. He was still for a moment, not speaking.

"The fates aren't here," Purvis said.

Eck looked up. "Out to lunch. We better move."

As Eck stood dressing himself, I noticed how his legs and fingers trembled. Purvis handed him a comb, and he wet his hair at the sink to slick it back, then carefully groomed his thin mustache. He was still enough of a cop to love crime (he told me once that if I ever wanted to rob something to head for a liquor store instead of a bank, and to wear a loud, ugly tie, which the victims would remember instead of my face), and he insisted on stuffing the bedclothes with his pillows to look like a body asleep. Then we made the elevator past the nurses' station and were out the electric doors of Baptist Hospital.

Back at the Robert E. Lee, Eck pulled his ten-speed bike down from its hooks and mounted it in the center of the room, balancing on the thin tires. He bought the bike the same week he quit smoking cold turkey, two days after my mother died. At first he pedaled the bike through the streets of downtown Winston wearing his Sansabelts and tan Hushpuppies, wobbling around corners. By the time my troubles began he had graduated to slick black biking shorts, wraparound sunglasses, and a leather helmet. He was winning his age group in local road races and being written up on the sports page.

Purvis fed strips of beef jerky to Desdemona, after admonishing me to stop clapping my hands to make her faint. I couldn't help myself; it was a neat trick. Purvis scratched her behind the ears.

"Well, Eck," he said, "you've world enough and time, what do you propose?"

Eck winced as he dismounted the bike. "Bedsores," he said to me. I learned he had been in the hospital not just a few days, as I imagined, but nearly two weeks. Long enough for his doctors to decide that his cancer was inoperable. When he coughed, the sound was like wringing water from a heavy sponge onto the sidewalk.

"Lily will find us here," Eck said.

"Let her," I said. "You have your rights. If you don't want to go back, tell her to go to hell."

"Well spoken," Purvis said.

"You don't understand, Robert," Eck said. He walked across the room to look at the retirement photo of himself standing with Clay Williams, the chairman of Reynolds Tobacco. In 1947 Eck left the police force in Washington and moved south, to be near his sisters. He found a job with Reynolds, where for the next twenty-eight years he operated a Molins cigarette-making machine, days spent packing Camels and Winstons and Salems in the Number 12 plant downtown.

Eck turned and looked at us. "Lily hammered on me, boys," he said. "I was doped up and sick, and I signed it all away. Wills and testaments, bank accounts, power of attorney, everything." He hesitated. "She can make me go back."

I shook my head. "And I'm saying I won't let her do that."

"Your place is here," Purvis said, as if that settled the matter. He didn't look up, but sat feeding handfuls of peanuts to Desdemona. "The question stands," he said, "what do you want to do?"

"Everything," Eck said. "But first I'd like to rest awhile." He lay back on the cot and coughed as if his lungs would tear apart.

Purvis petted Desdemona and whispered into her ear: "Easy now, girl. It scares me too."

Purvis and I watched his black and white TV, following the soap operas (a habit I'd picked up living alone) while Eck slept fitfully. The phone rang. When I answered it, Lily started in on me.

"I'm surprised at you, Robert. No wonder Deborah kicked you out."

"Don't start that," I said.

"Is Purvis behind all this? You tell him it's none of his business." She hesitated, and I didn't say anything. I realized as she said it that Purvis *was* behind all of this, that if it had been left to me, Eck would still be at the hospital.

"You'll kill him doing this," she said. "He'll run out of his pain medicine. I'm coming down there."

"Don't do it, Lily. He wanted out. Leave him in that hospital and you'll kill him sure enough."

"I'll call the police, Robert. I swear to God I will."

Eck stirred and coughed. "I'm sorry, Lily," I said, and hung up the phone, my hands shaking.

Twenty minutes later we were heading out of downtown in my Escort wagon, toward the highway. I kept watching in my rearview mirror. Eck said that he wanted to eat some real food for once and drink a beer and a cup of black coffee. He directed us to Harper's Cafe, where we drank bottomless cups and ate something called Pork Midnight, which Purvis called manna from heaven.

Afterwards, Eck decided we should get our beer by way of the free tour at the Schlitz brewery. I felt like we were school kids on some vice-ridden field trip. I parked near the loading dock, where shiny, battered kegs sat stacked on pallets. On the roof of the Schlitz plant was a mechanical billboard, so high up I had to crane my neck to see it. We faced the back of it, the unpainted side, but I knew what was around front. I'd seen it a thousand times, the bright young man, straight out of 1950 with his starched white shirt and crewcut, his arm working up and down, lifting over and over to his smiling red mouth an enormous bottle of Schlitz. When I was a kid and we'd drive past on the highway, Eck would nudge me and point to the sign.

"That fella's always thirsty," he'd say. "Never gets enough." That afternoon he'd forgotten to say it. I remembered bringing Debbie out along the highway to show her the billboard. I used Eck's line, to try to pry a laugh out of her. This was nearing the end of our marriage, before the real trouble started, but bad enough that I felt awkward around her half the time, this woman I'd slept with for ten years. She said only that the sign was an eyesore, and they ought to tear it down. I told her she was probably right.

We toured the plant wearing hard hats they gave us, while a heavy-set man in short sleeves and a clip-on tie explained the workings of the stainless vats and the vacuum pumps and the capping machines that whirred and hissed in the huge room below us. Purvis began lecturing the man about the Egyptian origins of the brewer's art. In the pale fluorescent light I noticed that Eck's arms and legs were colored with bruises, the blood spreading under his skin. He stopped and leaned against the rail. All his life he'd had an affection for machinery—guns, motorcycles, power tools, and finally bicycles—but now I knew something was wrong. He drew deep breaths, his eyes closed, his hands gripping the rail. I thought that all of this was too much like the hospital: the tile floors, stainless steel polished to a cold shine, workers in white uniforms. I moved beside him and took his arm, ready to lead him out of there. He held his ground and pressed his hand against the small of my back.

"Smell that, Robert," he said.

I imitated him, closing my eyes and opening my lungs to whatever he was smelling with his own ragged breaths. I hadn't noticed before—everywhere, pushing at the walls and the high ceilings, was the heavy odor of fermenting yeast. I breathed again, the smell as fertile as a sweaty greenhouse, rank as damp sheets after sex. A seed tossed into that thick air might have taken root.

"That's what we came here for," Eck said.

"It's nice," I agreed.

He was quiet a minute, breathing. "So she's gone for good?" he asked.

I almost laughed. "Yes," I said. "This one's pretty much over."

He nodded. "She seemed like a good girl. I'm no expert at marriage."

"I've always thought you and Purvis have a kind of marriage, a good one."

His eyebrows drew together.

"You know what I mean," I said. "You get along. You like each other."

Eck nodded. "Never thought much about it, to tell you

the truth. He's honest, pays his half of the rent." He seemed embarrassed, and for a moment I was jealous of the ease with which they'd carried out their twenty-year friendship.

"Women are a whole different ball game," he said.

"Amen to that."

At the end of the tour they gave us free samples of beer drawn from oak casks. Purvis sipped, swishing the beer in his mouth to taste it. Eck drank in gulps, the beer running out the edges of his mug down the front of his cycling shirt. We were silent awhile, drinking. Purvis read the pamphlets the man had given us, and he and Eck shared inside jokes and old drinking stories, their laughs echoing around us. Finally Eck wiped his mouth and looked at Purvis and me. "Don't let them put me back," he said.

By late afternoon Purvis was worried about Desdemona and took a taxi back to the hotel to feed her and change her litter box. He promised to play dumb if Lily called, and to meet up with us later. We decided we would be okay for a few hours at my place, the one house on a dead-end street near the bad part of town. The house sat in the shadow cast by the big screen of the X-rated drive-in. It had been leased to me for fifty bucks a month and the promise to bring the roof and foundation and plumbing up to code, which I had never much done. I moved in there the same day Debbie asked me to leave our house. At the time I imagined living in squalor as an act of revenge.

As we walked from the driveway to the house, Eck had to stop every few feet to rest. He would cough and spit blood, and push me away if I tried to help. He still wore his black biking shorts, and had his sunglasses sitting atop his head, in among the wet strands of his hair. I later found out he had refused chemotherapy, not wanting to lose his mustache. It seemed a worthy enough thing to hold onto.

Inside, he first noticed the wall of Bic pens, the separation papers and old letters stuck there, the dusty plaster powdering the floor.

"What the hell is all this, Robert?"

"Steam worked off," I said.

He nodded. "Better than firing a gun. You going to be all right with this?"

"I am," I said, though at that point I was still phoning Debbie nearly every night, sometimes just to hear her voice and then hang up while she said, *"Damn* it, Robert, I *know* it's you."

Eck noticed the column of figures I'd run, the account of all the money I lacked.

"This is no good," he said.

"I know."

"I mean if this is how you're going about it, you're lost."

I nodded, knowing he was right, and knowing at the same time that I would still send to Debbie the sapphire necklace I'd bought for her birthday and that she would send it back unopened.

Eck fell asleep in my bed, and I sat on the porch sipping the good bourbon I'd done without for those months leading up to the divorce. An empty conciliatory gesture on my part, as if I could pour my problems down the drain or stop buying them at the drive-up window. Drink was not what was wrong, but you grab what ballast you can. I watched stray shafts of light spear over the top of the high movie screen. I pulled a Camel filter from the pack in my jeans pocket and lit it, pulling the first drag deep into my lungs. All day I'd been itchy for a cigarette, but had put it off.

Behind me, Eck slept uneasily, moaning and grunting, his breath halting. I stubbed out my cigarette against my shoe and then said the word out loud: "Cancer." I said it to the porch rail, to the moths that circled above me, then threw my whiskey glass out into the dark yard where the light didn't reach.

A nighttime chill settled in, damp and airy. With my eyes closed, I could just make out the soundtrack carrying over from the drive-in, the moans of big-screen sex crackling out through tiny window speakers into the cars of those I imagined as lonely people. I thought of Debbie, incapable of loneliness. It had been two months now since I'd seen her, though as I say I still phoned her nearly every night. She would talk to me as if I'd called to sell her something, which in a way I had. On bad nights, after a few rounds of bourbon, I'd end up telling her I still loved her, and she got to sound superior and pitying, and I'd point that out and she would hang up. I heard from someone that she'd cut her hair.

The sound from the drive-in quit and the light ended, the nine o'clock show over. Darkness fell around me, and I wondered where all this dodging of the sisters was taking us, if finally Eck would have to go back even while hating it, his last wish not to. Lily had mentioned pain medication, and hearing Eck's fitful sleep, I knew she'd been truthful about it, that he needed more than the pills he'd brought. Eck coughed and moaned. Across the way, I heard cars leaving the gravel lot of the drive-in, carrying people home. I went inside and phoned Debbie.

"These calls have to stop eventually," she said. "You have to let go and embrace other possibilities." She was seeing a therapist at the university.

"Eck's sick," I said. "He's dying."

"What's wrong? Where is he?" It was good to again hear sympathy in place of the usual pity in her voice, to imagine part of it for me.

"He has cancer, and he's here with me."

"Shouldn't he be in the hospital?"

"He was. I took him out."

"God, Robert, can you do that?"

"Where would you rather be if you were dying?"

She was silent a moment. "Okay, I understand. But . . . well, do you need me to do anything?"

This seemed like an opening, a way for me to invent a reason for seeing her, for us to spend time together, drawn into his dying. But no pretext would come to me; there was only Eck in my bed, his fits of painful coughing, and what time he had left.

"Thanks anyway," I said.

Near midnight a taxi pulled up in front of the house, and Purvis stepped out. He walked into the yellow light of the porch wearing a hat with a tiny red feather stuck in the band. He was out of breath. At the kitchen table he downed half a cup of coffee before he spoke.

"Lily came by the hotel. She's threatening legal intervention again. My guess is she's serious."

"We didn't break any laws," I said.

Eck swung his legs out of bed and slowly sat up. "She'll draft her own laws and have them passed by Congress if she has to."

"Power of attorney," Purvis said. "She can get a court order tomorrow morning. She can have you committed if she wants to. 'In the interest of your well-being' was how she phrased it."

"This is a bunch of damn foolishness," Eck said, his

breath raspy. "Robert, if you take me to one more place then I'll call Lily and we'll work something out."

"Eck, you don't have to go to the hospital," I said.

Purvis nodded. "If need be, we'll arm ourselves with an attorney." He set his hat on the table.

"Damn right," I said. "If there's one thing I learned—"

"No." Eck stood. "I have to go back."

By this time, he said, he'd taken all his pills and had started on the handful of aspirin I kept in a shoebox in the bathroom. But he said that the aspirin was thinning his blood, that there was new bleeding in his bowels and in his cough.

"What's the brave thing? Die at home?" he said. Purvis and I said nothing.

"This pain's not getting any better," Eck said. He looked at the floor, as if embarrassed to admit pain.

"So where's this place you want to go?" I asked, thinking of Washington, the beat around Pennsylvania Avenue and Dupont Circle Eck had walked during the Depression, or even the White House, where he'd guarded Roosevelt and once played cribbage with the president in the Rose Garden. Those were the times out of which Eck brought the stories I remembered, the photographs he passed around and carried in his wallet. Washington was a six-hour drive away. I knew he would never make it. The pain of all those miles would be too much.

"I'd like to see the Reynolds Tobacco Company, Robert," he said. "The Number 12 plant downtown."

It had been eight years since Reynolds moved its corporate headquarters to Atlanta (the day the news hit the papers, Eck paced the hotel room shouting: "Bastards, bastards, *bastards.* You think they'll rename their damn cigarettes 'Atlantas'?"). The work of all the old factories moved to new computer-run facilities out in Tobaccoville and Clemmons. All of the red-brick plants had been left abandoned downtown.

"I thought you were going to tell me you wanted to see Washington," I said.

Eck shook his head. "That job was like eating your dessert first. Riding around on a motorcycle, marching in parades." He shook his head. Purvis nodded.

"But Reynolds is closed," I said.

"I'd guess there's a hundred ways in and out of that building. We used to call them coffee-break exits." He smiled. "Trust me," he said.

The chain link fence around Number 12 lay broken in half a dozen places, the NO TRESPASSING signs bent and rusted. Plywood boards had been cut to fit inside the brick window frames, and the front doors were chained and padlocked. The pavement around the building was spattered white with the droppings of pigeons that roosted in the exhaust grates of the ventilation fans. Eck pointed to a window beside the last platform of the fire escape. When I climbed up and pushed, the window pivoted open. I looked inside, at the factory lit here and there by shaded bulbs that hung down on long cords from the rafters. It smelled like someone's attic. I was startled to see the machinery still in place. I eased through the window and found footing on a narrow ladder mounted on the wall, then climbed down and pried open one of the big delivery doors for Eck and Purvis.

"Never heard it so quiet," Eck said. Our entry had stirred a layer of dust from the floor, swirling it into truncated cones around the shaded bulbs. The machines were covered with streaks of dust-filled oil and rust. I shouted *hello* to hear the echo.

Purvis cleared his throat. "It's interesting that many trace the origins of the Industrial Revolution to the early perfection—" He glanced at Eck and was quiet.

Eck turned and stood a moment, then moved away from us, rubbing the back of his neck. We followed, not speaking. The gray machines filled the room, several hundred of them in neat rows, like pianos in a warehouse. Eck moved along the row of machines, touching each one as he came to it.

"Paul Holcomb, Mark Vernon, Lee Hines, Tim Lewey, Bill Tatum, J. T. Reid," he said, naming the men who had run the machines. He stopped at the next-to-last one in the row and thumped it with his knuckles. "Eck Voight," he said.

He walked around his machine three times, wincing as he bent to peer underneath. He fingered the gears and spit on the glass dials to wipe them clean with his thumb.

"A thousand smokes a minute," he said. "How many is that times eight hours a day for twenty-eight years?" I could see Purvis doing the math in his head. Behind one machine was a wheeled canvas trolley, cut tobacco still left in the bottom. Eck lifted a clump of it, sniffed it and made a face, then dumped it into the hopper of the making machine.

"Fix those rusted parts, calibrate it, and this thing could work good as new," he said. He tapped the machine with his fist. "Crank it up and roll a tray full. Wouldn't that be something."

"No cure for obsolescence," Purvis said. Then he flushed and looked away for having said it.

I heard the cops before I saw them—the jingle of key rings, the squeak of leather holsters. I pulled Eck and Purvis by their arms and headed out of the light. Eck led us to a corner behind a brick furnace. We watched the two cops walk out of the next room, their radios squawking. In the dim light their badges glinted and the beams of their flashlights cut all around us.

Eck leaned toward me. "Sorry, Robert," he whispered. "No run left in me."

"They'll assume we're juveniles, that we've high-tailed it," Purvis said. "You watch." And we stood, waiting for what he said to come true. In the dark, Eck's eyes shone; I heard Purvis breathing behind me. The cops tried the doors, shined their flashlights into the rafters, and then left. We heard them drive away.

We walked back into the faint light. "We'd better move along now," Eck said.

"I think so," Purvis answered.

"Hold it," I said. I put my hand on the making machine, the pale green paint cool and slick. "You said you wanted to make a cigarette, I think you ought to make one."

Eck shook his head. "First off, there's no paper in the rollers, no blade in the cutter, and the moisteners are dried up."

"Then we'll just run the damn thing, for the sound of it." I grabbed the red handle on the side of the machine and pulled the rusted switch to ON. Nothing.

"This plant went power off eight years ago, Robert," Eck said. "You're smarter than that."

I worked the lever back and forth, then put my ear to the power box. I heard a faint hum, like a wasp trapped inside.

"It's got juice," I said. I leaned against the machine and slid my hands between the rollers under the hopper, trying to force them. My hands slipped out, black with oil and dust. I jimmied the switch again, banged it with my fist, then stretched fully across the line of rollers and wedged my hands in as far as I could, pulling until I shook, breathing the burned oil smell of the machine. My fingers began to slip, and then I felt Eck's hands grip my shoulders and jerk me backward.

"What in hell is wrong with you, Robert? If that thing did crank up, you'd lose half your goddamn arm."

I wiped my face on my sleeve.

"Just leave it alone," Eck said. His voice echoed. I hadn't seen him as angry since I was fifteen and he caught me cheating at poker. We stood there in the quiet.

Purvis cleared his throat. "Well," he said.

My hands shook and I pushed them into the pockets of my jeans, nearly crushing my cigarettes.

"Wait a minute," I said. I took the bent pack of Camel filters from my pocket, shook one out, and offered it to Eck.

"It's an Atlanta cigarette," I said. For a minute he looked at me, then he took the cigarette and studied it, held it familiarly between his two fingers where the nicotine stains had long since faded. He sniffed it, broke off the filter, and lifted the cigarette to his mouth.

"Fire it up," he said.

I lit it for him, cupping the match the way he'd shown me twenty years earlier. The tip flared, the paper crackling and falling away in ash. Eck pulled deep and held it, suppressed a cough, then exhaled as fully as he could, the cloud of smoke twisting in rags.

"Good as the first one?" I asked.

"Better," Eck said. "It's the last one."

He laughed, threw the cigarette to the concrete floor, and stamped it out.

"Let's get the hell out of here," he said. He lifted his arm around my shoulder, his motion scattering the last tatters of smoke like he'd chased them away.

* * *

Eight months after we buried Eck, I drove downtown to the Robert E. Lee and found Purvis, still the same, milking Desdemona. He answered the door with his shirt sleeves rolled up.

"Trying my hand at cheese making," he said. "An ancient art, Robert. My eyes won't let me read much anymore." On the floor sat a copper bucket with an inch of the milk in the bottom. Desdemona stood sniffing the hot plate. Purvis moved around the room straightening piles of books, stuffing trash into his pockets. A fan rotated on top of the TV, the breeze from it slowly turning the front wheel of Eck's bike, still suspended from the ceiling.

"I wanted to see how you're doing," I said. I felt awkward, standing with this man I'd known for seventeen years.

"You're not remarried are you?"

"Not yet," I said, as if I had any prospects. I had last spoken to Debbie three months before, drunk one night, a conversation that showed me only that I had nothing left in me to say to her. I hung up and, staggering, penciled in a hundred zeros beside the last dollar figure at the baseboard, then pulled out all the Bic pens and put them away.

"Are you strong, Robert?" Purvis asked. I thought he meant emotionally, following the divorce, Eck's death.

"Yes, Purvis. I'm fine."

"But are you *strong?* Make a muscle."

He felt my muscle, such as it is. "You'll do," he said. "I have a bad tooth and I want you to pull it."

I looked at him. "Purvis—I don't—I think you'd better see a dentist."

"I've seen him. I need a tooth pulled. I paid for a diagnosis, why not hire on the muscle gratis?"

I suspected that he hadn't seen a dentist, that rent increases were eating up his Social Security, that he was living on goat cheese and the cooking sherry he was drinking.

"What would I have to do?" I said.

From a cigar box filled with pliers, scissors, and picture hangers he pulled out an antique dental tool, which looked like an old iron corkscrew but with a hook at the end. "Tooth extractor," he said. "Picked it up at a flea market."

Before I had a chance to speak, he poured sherry over the hook and began packing his cheek with Kleenex.

"One quick turn and the damn thing's out," he said, his voice muffled. He sat in a straight chair, leaned back his head, and opened his mouth, exposing his yellowed, cracked teeth. He pointed to the bad one, the gum below it red and swollen. I had to fight the urge to walk out and leave him there. Purvis positioned the extractor against his tooth, the handle sticking out of his mouth like a propeller. He braced his hands on the chair and looked up at me. I took a breath, gripped the handle of the extractor, then held steady the side of his head and twisted. Purvis grunted and shut his eyes. Blood soaked into the Kleenex. The extractor handle refused to move, like it had been cast in cement. I tightened my grip on the extractor and tried again. Just as I decided to give up, his jaw popped, the tooth tore loose of its flesh, and blood pooled in the space beneath his tongue. He went into the bathroom where I heard him spit and rinse.

I stood next to Eck's cot and petted Desdemona, the extracting tool in my hand. On the floor between my feet was the tooth, bloody and pulpy.

"Sit, Robert," Purvis said from the bathroom. "Let me pour you a sherry."

Before I sat, I took up his rotted tooth from the floor and

started cleaning it with my handkerchief. Purvis walked out of the bathroom, fresh blood in the corners of his mouth.

"You'll stay, won't you?" Purvis asked.

"Here it is," I said. I held the tooth out to him, and he squinted to look at it. It had shined up like a seashell, yellowed and scarred, jagged against my palm. I looked around at all the things Purvis had saved, and knew he would want to keep this as he had kept his trick ashtrays and globe banks and books, Eck's clothes and bicycle. I thought of such things that are kept, or lost, or happened upon by accident. I lifted the tooth to the light.

"Can I keep this?" I said.

Clown Alley

NED Samuelson is his real name. Every two hours I part his toes and push a needle through his skin, his veins as familiar to me as my own. He uses up his days shriveled in vinegar bedding. The nalprozene runs the streams of his blood, empties into his brain. He rides away his hurt. There are days I let it get to me, let this dust and wet stench choke me. I choke on the ragged life Ned clings to, on not taking myself out of here for good. Then the alarm on my watch beeps, and I withhold his needle. Ten minutes, fifteen. The game into overtime. Ned watches while I toss the glass syringes into the wall filled with yellowed eight-by-tens, the glossy photos of Emmet Kelly, Otto Griebling, Lou Jacobs,

Paul Jerome. The greats, Ned calls them, the gods. Dead, they love him in faded autographs. The syringes quiver in their vaudeville faces. Ned raises himself on shaky arms.

"Now, Johnny," he says. "Right now, the shot, or you're nothing, you never work again." His voice runs thin. "Please," he says, "the needle. Don't wait." An angel of mercy, I part his toes. If I withheld for a day, he'd shatter.

He circles my neck with his arms and I lift him, the skin casing his bones threatening to tear. The smell in his mouth is black. I stand him behind his walker, help him move to the window so he can look down at the passing lunchtime crowd and wave. The brats from his Yahoo Brigade are all grown up now, fat and balding, oily-haired in cheap suits, the women in pants hiding C-section scars and spider veins. Ned stares, propped by the aluminum tubing. I know in his fragile mind the people gather to cheer him, the famous tramp clown, waving the Hobo Ned hats and Hobo Ned plastic cigars they've kept all these years in shoeboxes, in the dark corners of attics. They are all ten years old again, bleached angel children in crinoline and clip-ons, cast in waves through the air on live TV, from studio bleachers to boxy Philcos, and set down through the years below our windows, on the sidewalk across from the Plasma Center.

"They don't forget," Ned says. He looks at me, eyes gone milk. "Twenty-three years I'm off the air, and who says I'm nobody? You tell me, Johnny." He bends in blood coughs, wheezing at the tube in his neck.

"What's the big deal?" I say. "Lawyers and secretaries out for lunch, they see some crazy old bastard at an apartment window, and they wave. So what?"

"So what the hell do you know? You work for me, doc. Understand? You know what I tell you to know. You want

to go across the street and sell blood to buy your dope?" His walker scrapes, stirring layers of dust.

He's figured it out about me, the H I buy on Lombard Street. Not enough to feed a habit. I have a small itch and I scratch, nights when Ned is sleeping and the syringes are cold in the walls. And I'm no doctor. Two years as a medtech taught me to pop a bleeder. Stealing from hospital pharmacies put me on the street for a while. A vein collapsed and I lost the tip of my little finger. I can feel the finger still there, throbbing, tickling. Push the plunger and you say, *I want.* My veins, pumping through those empty hours, grow hungry. I feed them like babies.

Ned taunts me with big promises, all his shopping-mall and racehorse money one day raining on me. Like buckets of confetti, he tells me, that old gag. I pass for family. No one else is left alive to name in his will. While he's asleep I search the place, turning up bankbooks, notarized certificates, old bond issues, nothing hard.

We share two rooms above the Carolina Theatre, where Hobo Ned first got his start in the business. So now he's come back here to die. In the corner of the big room stands a television camera, black matte and chrome, laced with cobwebs, bent like a giant at the neck. Camera One from Ned's first morning cartoon show at WFMY. Among my many duties—buying mackerel in sour cream, emptying bedpans—is keeping the lens of the camera polished up. Ned finds his reflection there and smiles at the world. At night the broken glass of marquee bulbs shines like ice on the tar paper roof below us, the streets empty, the buildings around us boarded up. Dead town. Across from us, winos line up to sell their blood. I watch, sleeping in snatches on the window seat, feeding him oxygen when he rattles.

From above drifts down the dirty fluff of pigeon nests. I bend over Ned, touch my ear to his chest, stroke his parchy skin, breathing his ammonia. "Anytime," I whisper into his sleep, "I could leave you."

Restoration begins on the Carolina Theatre, filling our days with the noise of power saws and hammers. The vibrations below us push the dust to the corners of our rooms, shake chalk from the sheetrock. Camera crews arrive from the local TV news. Ned wants the needle every half-hour, so he can stand and watch the trucks pulling in. He pays me extra and I shoot him up. I lift him like something to drape around me, get him to the window. He pulls his old top hat from the wall and wears it to wave at the work crews. They laugh, turn their faces up to him. It's 1954 again. Ned's pale eyes dilate. I spend the money on Lombard Street, two bills bet on a white horse.

The newspaper runs file photos of Ned in the early days at the Carolina, the sad clown with his hat and cigar, his fingerless gloves, tattered clothes, and two-string mop, painted-on stubble and a broken heart. Ned has me cut out the article and tape it to the wall, where the old ones curl and yellow.

The day after the photos appear, a woman calls to ask Ned to cut the ribbon on stage at the restored Carolina, where he got his start doing bicycle lotteries, juggling cigar boxes at Saturday matinees. The woman asks me if Ned will need a wheelchair ramp to the stage, if he has any "special needs."

"Like what, for instance?" he says when I repeat her question to him. "A pine box? Brass urn for my ashes?" He decides to surprise them all, to stand and give them the full seven minutes of his old mop routine.

"My makeup kit," he says. "Find it. I have to rehearse."

Everything here is preserved: the camera, dirty mirror framed by lights, mahogany wardrobe. Clown alley held in dust. The latches on the makeup kit are rusted shut. I snap them and open the box, releasing the smell of greasepaint and spirit gum, still fresh and wet after eighteen years.

Ned smears his face with the pancake, and the whiteness of it makes his eyes look yellow. It bleeds into the fringes of his brown hair, stops at the wattles of his neck. He lifts a grease pencil to trace his eyebrows, to outline his sad hobo frown. The sleeve of his pajama top slips down to his elbow. He shakes, holding one hand with the other.

"I can't," he says. He looks at me, his mouth a wound in his white face. "You'll have to do it," he says.

"I don't want to, so forget it."

"But you will, Johnny. You'll do it whether you want to or not. Now get your ass over here."

I look at him, thinking of Lombard Street, the needles in the wall. His lips move like gills. Beneath the grease pencil his skin feels wooden, slick from the pancake. From the posters around us I make his face, fill in his eyebrows, trace the wide frown around his mouth, blacken his lips, redden the tip of his nose. It is Hobo Ned, looking as if he could still do his backflip or chase baby chicks around the soundstage. Twenty-three years erased.

He looks at himself in the makeup case mirror. "Not bad, Johnny boy. You're a natural." Shrunk in his bed, all made up, he looks like a bad dream.

He asks for a shot. "Make it a double," he says, and I oblige, hoping it won't kill him, hoping it will. The nalprozene filters through him and I lift him from bed. He stands without the walker, held by the drug. From the wall he pulls down the two-string mop, the act that made him famous on the *Red Skelton Show*.

After I juice him up we make the walk down the hall to the freight elevator. The hall is full of dust and graffiti, the walls peeling, the floor dotted with moths and rat shit. We find our way to the stage and Ned limps across with his two-string mop, wearing a topcoat over his pajamas, leaving his trail in the sawdust.

"You got a part in this," he says to me. "My stooge." His voice echoes in the empty hall. On the ceiling are tangles of wire where the lighting fixtures will go. "You get paid double," he says.

"What do I have to do?"

"Here's the sketch. I work in this pet shop as a janitor, right? We need a big sign says 'Pet Shop.' I'm mopping around, cleaning up dog hair or whatever, then I pantomime dropping and breaking my specs. That's the set-up, you with me?"

"So far."

"Then you come from the wings carrying a big box marked 'Poultry' and you trip and let these baby chicks run loose. A hundred or so. My glasses are busted, so I think the chicks are dust balls or whatever, and I chase them all over hell trying to clean them up with this crummy mop. You try and stop me, and by the blow-off I'm after *you* with the mop."

"Sounds hilarious."

"It's a great gag, let me tell you, bub. A classic." From somewhere in the hall sounds the pounding of a hammer.

"Where are we supposed to get baby chicks?" I ask.

He hasn't thought of this. For a moment, his eighty-three years bleed through the makeup.

"Besides that," I tell him, "they won't allow it. The animal rights people."

"Animal rights? You're shitting me." He sits on the stage, wheezing in the dust. I wonder if he might lie down and die right here. His bony ankles stick out of the cuffs of his pajama pants. He doesn't move.

"Listen," I say. "What about ping-pong balls?" Ned looks up at me. "The sign says 'Sporting Goods' and I spill a box of ping-pong balls?"

Without my help, he stands, and walks over to pat my cheek. "You got a future, kid," he says.

Back at the room, he is wound up and will not sleep. There is tingling in my hands, my lips numb.

"I'm going out," I say. "You lay down and I'll give you a pill to put you out." We no longer keep any schedule with his medications. Downstairs the workers have quit for the day; there is silence and the smell of turpentine.

"No time. We're in the rushes now, pal," Ned says to me. From his night table he withdraws a cigar and lights it, striking the match on his iron bed frame, using his thumb to plug the tube in his neck so he can inhale.

"We got rehearsals. Somebody—you—has to feed me straight lines. I met Chaplin once in New York. He told me, you practice till it looks like falling off a log."

"Sorry, Ned. I have to go." My lips buzz. My hands, the joints of my fingers feel elongated, stretching out the way nights do when Ned is wheezing and I am alone watching Lombard Street, watching light pool on the darkened windows of the Plasma Center and thinking about the frozen bags of blood inside. When the itch grows, you need a bigger scratch. I follow my hand to the knob while Ned watches me. The room is cold.

"I want you to stay," Ned tells me. The makeup looks as

if it has slid on his face. He raises his hand and pulls money out of the air, tosses it to me. The hundred-dollar bills flutter down.

"Give me one hour, doc," he says, "then you're welcome to go out and kill yourself." We rehearse until he falls asleep, which every night seems more like he is passing into a coma. The pancake and black frown smear gray across his pillow. I take the bills from the floor and go.

The next morning he is hard to wake. The shots pass right through him. With a stiff rag and a jar of cold cream I wipe away his makeup. The clown-white fills the tiny cross-hatched ridges in his skin. My own arms are dotted with yellow bruises inside the elbow. I finish cleaning him up, rolling him to change the sheets and wipe away his bile. He sleeps during it all, wheezing through his tube. I sit on the edge of his bed and watch him. With my thumb I plug the tube, hold it closed till he begins to quiver, then pull my hand away. "I keep you alive," I say. I hold his hand till his eyes flutter open.

He looks at me. "What's your name, young soldier?" he says. I feel bad for taking away his makeup, giving him back his old age.

"Don't have a name, Hobo Ned. I sold it." Slowly his fog lifts and his eyes dish around the room, his posters, dead friends, his old life.

"The shot," he says.

"Stabbed you right before you woke up, boss. Give it a few." He closes his eyes and winces.

"Tell me again," he says.

"You remember. You got a gig. Ribbon cutting downstairs and everybody turning out to see you before you die."

"You talk out your ass," he says. "I'll outlive you, and you'll never see a dime."

I squeeze his hand and he calls me a fairy. His pupils are turning the color of eggshell.

"Hey, listen," he says. "Man walks into a bar, he's got a duck shoved down the front of his pants . . ." His words melt into slur, and he sleeps.

Nights after my visits to Lombard Street, the veins in my arms won't shut. The blood, unable to clot, runs in thin ribbons over my clothes while I sleep. In the mornings I clean myself up, shivering, praying not to lose another finger. The money gives out while my arms are still hungry. After Ned passes into his nightly coma, I turn the rooms out, searching for the stash he keeps drawing out of thin air with his parlor trick bribes. I peel the walls and pry up loose floorboards, search his pockets, his dresser drawer, the wardrobes and makeup tables in clown alley. Nothing turns up but dust, old playbills, wingtip shoes and dark suits, a smell of loose tobacco and mothballs, of burnt cork and greasepaint.

I can only wake him now with a fat shot of the nalprozene; I have long since stopped measuring out the cc's. The drug is fouling the work of his brain as he spirals down larger doses. Awake, he can move without the walker now, sweep the stage with his two-string mop during rehearsals, even manage a tottering soft-shoe. He is numbness walking, the pain washed out of him.

"I need more money," I tell him. There is a looseness in my bowels, and I try to think how long it has been since I have thought of food.

"You're dropping weight," he says, as if reading my

mind. "You look worse than I do, like you're a ghost or something."

"I said I need cash, Ned. I'll fucking walk out of here."

"Shut your hole, Casper, and get me the makeup kit. We need to rehearse. I can't remember anything."

"No. More bread. Cough it up." As I say it, he bends forward in the bed and coughs into his sheet. The stain left there is dark red.

"Hey, good one there, Casper. I oughta start charging you for straight lines." He reaches into the night table drawer, draws out a cigar, and lights it. The smoke curls in bluish streamers toward the ceiling. He puffs again and the cigar explodes. From the ragged end he withdraws and unrolls a hundred-dollar bill.

"Now, get the makeup kit."

I take the kit from clown alley and set it on the bed beside him.

"Give me a shot, and do my face. When is the show? Tell me again."

"Day after tomorrow."

"Good. We got time." He pats the bed. "Sit here and do your job. I ever tell you the Hobo Ned face is legally mine? Any other clown ever uses my design, I can sue his ass here till Tuesday." I put the drug in his vein, and everything in him settles and relaxes. My hands shake worse than his.

"I have to go out," I say. The itch covers me like a fur coat.

"Like hell. We got work."

"I need more money." I toss the jar of pancake on the bed.

"I just gave you a c-note. You want dough every time you take a breath? Do my face, and be careful, do it right." He closes his eyes, presses his lips together.

"Forget it, Ned, I'm going out." I stand and move toward the door.

"You're going nowhere unless I say so." I pull open the door, and grit blows into my eyes. Ned raises himself in the bed.

"Don't come back if you leave here. I don't want to know you, I don't want to see your ugly mug. You're out of the will, not a dime." The tube in his neck faintly whistles as he breathes.

"Go on then and get the hell out of here. Go die, for what I care." His voice follows me through the thin wall and down the stairs into the street.

When I come back, my arms are bleeding, my head floating in jelly. Ned is asleep and wheezing, the jars and tubes of greasepaint scattered around the bed sheets. He has tried to do the makeup himself. His face is dashed with streaks of white, clumps of the pancake stuck in his hair. The darker colors smear along the front of his pajama top and across his shoulder. His chin instead of his nose is red. I can imagine his attempt, confused, his weak arms failing him, the tubes of paint dropping out of his reach. While he sleeps I fix his face, bring Hobo Ned back out of the mess.

When he wakes, I am holding his hand, touching the raised veins, the yellowed nails.

"I thought I told you not to come back."

I squeeze his fingers and laugh. "What would you do without me, old man? You wouldn't last a day."

"So you're laughing, funny boy? Let me tell you, when Ned Samuelson finishes business, he finishes business. Now get out, and stop leeching off me."

"You'll die, Ned. You'll never get through the show."

He angles the lid of the makeup kit so he can see himself

in the mirror. "Perfect," he says. "Did I need your help in '61, when I did Ed Sullivan? Up yours."

"Ned . . ."

"Out, loser, or I'll call the cops."

I stuff my things into a grocery sack and head out the door, taking as I go everything I can hock. The last thing I hear is Ned practicing his lines, getting all of them wrong, forgetting them in mid-sentence or interrupting himself with wet coughs.

I scrounge enough for a room, one of the dives on Lombard. Before I can get there I spend the money in the shadows, a quick, fat pop behind the dumpster. It is cold and damp out at night, the steam grates all taken. I walk, feeling my eyes move like eels, hearing the sound of blood in veins. I keep circling the block without meaning to. The time, the deadness of the night, seem to roll back and back on themselves, repeating like ocean waves.

By the time I make it back to Ned's I am out of money, and have lost somewhere my sack of clothes. The Carolina is polished up for the next day's ceremonies, the front of the building draped with a thick, red ribbon. Hobo Ned's name shines on the marquee. There is numbness in the tips of my fingers, moving up my arm.

Inside, Ned is on the bed, propped on the pillows, wearing his makeup. On the floor, in the light from the marquee, glitter the broken shards of a glass syringe and the nalprozene vial. Beside them, Ned's top hat has fallen out of his reach.

Ned has managed his makeup by himself, but again everything is wrong. This time he has forgotten the pancake completely, and has painted his mouth with a huge, white, maniac smile instead of his gray frown with the whiskers. The shaky, black outline of his smile extends to his cheekbones and below his chin. It takes up half of his face.

"You stupid old man," I say. "You don't even look like a hobo. You don't even look sad, for godsakes." He does not stir, and there is no nalprozene to rouse him. A strange noise invades the tiny room, and I realize it is the absence of the wheezing from the tube in Ned's neck. When I touch him he is stiff. My thumb on his tube makes no difference. I sit on the bed and lean across his lap for the rag and cold cream. In the tilted lid of the makeup kit, the streaked mirror catches my face, my own dark eyes. Instead of the cold cream I watch my fingers dip into the white pancake. For that moment I think of wearing it, of disappearing in the grease. Around me, the vaudeville faces look down at us. *A great gag,* they tell me, *a classic.* Their yellow glossy eyes never close.

Escaping

OCTOBER had arrived, the season of typhoid, when the women and children withered as quickly as leaves on the trees. All the beds and the overflow cots on the ward where Anna Privitte worked were full, the emaciated bodies in tremors, the blues and greens and browns of the children's eyes set like stones in their faces. For twenty hours she had sat with the boy, his name already lost to her, spooning him boiled eggs and stewed fruit, combing with her fingers his sweat-matted hair and cleaning the fever sores on his mouth, before the hemorrhaging finally took him. He died that morning with his fingers curled against his cheek.

She moved now through the early afternoon along Eutaw

Street toward Lexington Market, away from the hospital, drawing her cape tight to her against the autumn wind that found spaces in her shoes where the buttons had fallen away. Her back stiffened from the hours in the iron chair at the boy's bedside, her arms sore from turning him. In the streets around her the ladies from town in their finery alighted from carriages, followed by servants carrying baskets. A fat man with blond hair and thick mustaches touched Anna's arm. "Plump rabbits today, ma'am." His voice boomed. "Fresh killed, twenty-five cents." She frowned at him, pulling away from his touch, and drew off the sidewalk into the street, stepping between the drays loaded with barrels of oysters, with watermelon and lumber. Anna raised her hand to her mouth and nose against the smell of the coal oil lamps that burned for the Saturday night market. It was early, hours yet from dark. The boy's body would still be laid out in the hospital mortuary, where she, like every nurse, delivered her dead. In that tiny room with its stained-glass windows and terrible silences, she washed his papery skin, wrapped him in winding sheets, and covered his blank face.

In the street children darted between the legs of horses while the poor bartered for cuts of shin and neck and tail. Along the sidewalk people shouted in her ears, offering vegetables and butchered meats. Anna could not tolerate the crowds, the press of noise, the flies still thick this late in the year. She would go home to rest, and make do without the potatoes and cabbage and soup bones for the stew she and her mother shared. Most evenings they ate together standing in the kitchen, then let their food run cold while they practiced songs together or read books in the quiet house. They had lived this way since Anna was nine and her father had died of blood poisoning.

Lately, at night, she would be awakened in her bed by the

shouts of their new-married neighbors in the rowhouse next door, by the dull slam of Mrs. Dombrowski thrown against the wall. Anna was twenty-seven now, and when she closed her eyes to hear those thumps that rattled the pots from the kitchen shelves, she thought it just as well that she would never marry, that the chance would never arise. Already, the boys on the corners would whisper *old maid* as she walked past them toward the hospital, reaching out their greasy fingers for the touch of her skirts.

As she rounded the corner at Calvert Street, a crowd of people rushed past her, men pulling their women by the elbows, mothers snatching up their children, shouting at one another to hurry or they would miss the show. Before she could turn and start toward the alley the throng drew her in like fast water, her feet nearly lifted off the bricks. Elbows jabbed into her ribs, shoulders and hands buffeted her spine and trapped her arms by her sides. She felt the tug of her skirts as children bumped into her legs. She had to force herself to breathe. Someone shoved into her hands a pamphlet, *Harry Houdini: The Adventurous Life of a Versatile Artist*. As she slowed to read, she was butted across the back of her head by a forearm or elbow, her face smothered into the wool mackinaw of the man before her.

"Don't," she said. The harsh wool scratched her cheek as she fought to keep her footing beneath her. She pushed against the man to right herself, her cold face chafed and stinging. Beside her, a boy led a monkey tethered to a thin brass chain. She saw an elderly man drop his eyeglasses and reach for them as the crush of shoes and brogans took them. Discarded oyster shells broke against the paving stones beneath her feet. From the basin of Baltimore Harbor sounded the thunderclap of lumber being unloaded from ships and tossed in stacks on the docks. She focused on the sound as she gave herself up to the press of people. Strands of her hair came unpinned and fell around her face. Somewhere, she had lost her tulle cap.

The forward push of the crowd along Calvert Street slowed and then ceased, and here and there pockets of space opened. Anna moved toward one of these, where men stood circled, smoking cigars. She watched them count up bets, then fasten the money with a gold clip. They asked a boy to hold the pooled money, and he stuck it away inside his cap. The boy's face glowed with pink blotches across his cheeks. *Fever,* she thought, her breath catching, then realized it was only the boy's healthiness, his excitement. Around her, fingers pointed at the afternoon sky, and everyone there, the men and ladies and children, and even the stray dogs, looked up.

From a beam atop the Fidelity Building there hung a block and tackle, a braided rope that looped through the pulleys disappearing among the hats and oiled hair of the crowd. The rope tightened and quivered, a loud "Heave-ho!" rose up, and a voice laced with Scottish accent told everyone to "stand away, clear away." As the cadence rang out and the pulleys on the block and tackle scraped and whined, a man—Houdini, she realized—lifted up over the heads of the throng, tethered to the rope by his ankles, swaying. Anna raised her hands to her mouth. She watched this Houdini swing bound in a straightjacket, the brass buckles along his back glinting in the afternoon sun. She had seen the jackets before, men brought into the hospital chewing their tongues, shouting in spit and blood. Houdini's face darkened, and he spoke words she could not hear as the men let him down again. When the crowd pulled back, Anna found herself to be one of those forming the circle around Houdini. She turned to look behind her

toward town and saw nothing but faces; in the distance, boys and girls stood on the fenders of the automobiles.

"Now watch," Houdini said, his voice raspy with the constriction of his lungs from the canvas and leather bindings. "This you have not seen before."

He lay on his back, the rope holding his bare feet half a yard off the pavement. As he moved, Anna heard the buckles of the straightjacket scrape the cobbles beneath him. A thick-chested man, the man with the Scottish accent, snapped his fingers in the air and a younger man with browned, gaping teeth led forth a horse pulling a small dray. On the boards of the dray steamed a large copper kettle. Using his handkerchief, the young man lifted the pot handle and poured the steaming water over the straightjacket. Anna thought back to that morning, when she had carbolized the heavy rubber sheets from the boy's bed, her last task after every death.

"Be careful of his face, now, his legs," the Scotsman shouted. A steam cloud rose up with the smell of boiled cotton, and the dray horse snuffled and stepped. The water hissed as it ran between the cobbles, and the canvas of the straightjacket darkened with the wetting. Somewhere behind Anna, a woman said, "That'll shrink it right down." The men with cigars took back their money from the boy and strengthened their bets, counting the bills aloud, writing on slips of paper. Houdini directed his Scottish helper and two other assistants to hoist him back into the air. As he rose up, people in the crowd waved hats and handkerchiefs. A shower of brass souvenir coins rained down, and boys scrambled after them, tearing the knees of their pants. A short, skinny man leaned against Anna, laughing, smelling of whiskey and tobacco. She suppressed the urge to run away.

Houdini inched up fully the height of the building, twisting on the rope like a caught fish. People shielded their eyes against the bright sky. The men who had bet withdrew and opened their pocket watches. Houdini kicked against the air and fought the jacket in spasms that rang the block pulleys. The only sound now was silence, dimpled here and there by shouted encouragements and the chattering of the monkey hidden in the crowd. Anna looked around her, all the faces lifted. By now her mother would be praying out loud, frantic that Anna had not returned from work.

Then Anna noticed the Scotsman, watching her, his eyes narrowed. She felt herself blush, like a school girl caught daydreaming. She looked away and pulled the cape tight around her, the smells of the boy on her. When she turned back, the Scotsman still watched her, not smiling, his hat tipped back on his head, his silver hair even across his forehead, his face ruddy and jowly. Though she could not stand to look at him, neither could she make herself look away. She remembered, years before, the first dawn after the night of the Great Fire, when the sun lay buried in the smeared sky. Late that morning ambulances brought in the men hurt in an explosion at the Steiff Paint factory. The nurses worked cutting off the clothes of the men where the fabric had not melted to the skin. The men cried out, naked on their stretchers. Their cut-away leather aprons and suits, bright with the greens and blues of the explosion, red with their own blood, quilted the cold floor of the emergency area. Anna knelt among the men, her stomach buckling inside her. She bandaged a man who had lost his eyes to flaming turpentine, and was beside him a week later when the doctor removed the bandages and the man ran his fingers over his face, lightly, as if brushing away rain water. He heard her there and turned to the sound of her, his face peeled, his empty sockets inflamed tissue. He took up her hand in his.

"Please tell me you're pretty. A pretty girl," he said. She was seventeen then, and had worked as a probationer for only a week, sterilizing the towels and dressings and instruments in the operating room. He nodded a little, tilting his head. His fingers were calloused. He had been handsome. The doctor and head nurse smiled and nodded to her as well. She swallowed.

"No. I'm plain," she told him. "I'm an ordinary girl." She had dropped his hand then, she remembered, had run back upstairs to the children on her ward.

As Anna looked up, Houdini began swinging in a pendulum arc, his hair hanging down. Beneath the straightjacket he wore only a white bathing suit, the muscles in his thighs like the flanks of horses. Houdini strained and grunted, the cords in his neck thickening. His head jerked, and drops of moisture umbrellaed out to catch the afternoon light. As Anna began to believe he had made no progress in his escape, she saw his left arm slide further up under his armpit. He pushed again, spinning and huffing with each breath. The men with cigars tapped their pocket watches and passed around more money and shouted profanities. The Scotsman whispered into the ear of his assistant, his eyes still on her. She buried her hands in her cape. Houdini twisted and swayed, his white breath expelling in bursts. He looked in the rhythm of his struggles like some mechanical device, like the clocks her father had collected. As she watched, his elbow wrenched down across his face and his right arm pulled free.

The crowd started up its noise again and surged against her back. She heard in their words the twin hopes that he would escape and that he would not, that he would triumph from his efforts or die from them, dangling and spinning. She thought of the worst sound she'd heard in the hospital, at night on the women's ward during typhoid season, when the delirious asked for water they could not keep down by banging on their nightstands with tin cups. Banging until they wore down and gave up.

The sun pushed shadows from the scaffolded buildings surrounding the street, the repairs to the city ongoing still, ten years after the Great Fire. Houdini shouted as his other arm wrenched loose. He pulled with his teeth at the leather straps along his fists. His arms loosed from one another and the shouts in the crowd began to rise. Reaching behind he unhasped two of the buckles along his spine, pinching them through the stiff canvas. He swung out over the crowd, nearly hitting the Fidelity Building on backswings. He twisted once inside the straightjacket, and again, then the jacket pulled down off his shoulders and he was free of it, holding it by its sleeve and waving it at the crowd. The noise of the people rose up beyond hearing, the roar like water against her eardrums. Someone threw a bouquet of flowers; cap pistols popped, making the dogs bark. Houdini extended his arms and took his bow upside down in the air.

The circle pushed back as the assistants lowered Houdini to the cobbles and the men with cigars handed money around, wetting their fingers to count it. The crowd gathered tightly, straining to see, and the Scotsman shouted for his assistants to keep everyone back. Then Houdini leapt atop the dray, resting his bare foot on the handle of the copper kettle, and he tossed the straightjacket to the reporters standing about with their notebooks and flash cameras. He wore no shirt, only the white cotton bathing suit, and in the cold his skin puckered and turned red in blotches along his legs. His chest and shoulders had bruised from his struggle with the straightjacket, some of the bruises as wide as hands. Out of breath, he invited the reporters to inspect the jacket, to come collect a thousand-dollar reward if they found anything amiss. The cheers eased away and the people applauded now as if at the theatre, the boys jumping from the fenders of cars, some of the women crying. Without meaning to, Anna found herself applauding as well. Houdini shouted for all to return in two hours, a block away at water's edge where he would "challenge the icy depths of the harbor." Anna looked for the Scotsman, but he was gone.

The crowd shifted against one another and pressed toward Eutaw and Pratt streets, jostling her, milling about as if they did not know where to go, as if they had no homes or businesses to return to. She thought back to the cold night in February, ten years ago, when she had opened a curtain on E ward, thinking she heard ambulance bells, and had seen instead a spotted horse careening down the street dragging a milk wagon, the wagon riderless, milk jugs spilling on the pavement. In the next minute the streets filled with the noise of explosions and fire wagons, of window glass raining from the buildings downtown. All that night the flames spread, and people pressed into the streets in the freezing weather, standing behind the firelines the police had strung, the mist from the hoses freezing to ice on the power lines overhead, in the mustaches and fur collars of the watchers. The fire became a show, everyone cheering the blasting of dynamite or the extinguishing of small blazes, until from everywhere the smoke ran down in thick clouds like cable cars through the streets, and people moved to get away from it and there was no getting away. By morning of the third day the city smouldered, the skipjacks and steamers in the wharves bobbing in six inches of soot and ash as if thrown adrift in fields of dirty snow. Anna worked with the nurses and other probationers for three days straight, hearing stories the ambulance drivers told. One man, sitting at his desk in his office, had swallowed water from the fire hoses and drowned. A mother and child were found fused by the heat. In the days that followed the fire, people of the city had roamed the streets, looking over the ruin, watching the smouldering ash.

Anna walked quickly along South Street. As she found a pathway out of the milling crowd, a young man fell into step beside her and pressed his hand at the small of her back. She grabbed his arm to push him away.

"We'll need your help, miss. Over here." She thought that someone in the movement of the crowd had been injured and now required medical attention, but he steered her away from the crowd, down a narrow alley.

She stopped and jerked away from him. "What kind of help exactly?" she said. "Who are you?" She looked into his face and recognized him as one of Houdini's assistants, the one with the ruined teeth. She guessed him to be close to her own age.

"We just need you," he said, his eyes darting about. "Quickly."

He directed her into the lobby of the Altamont Hotel. The silence and solitude of the hotel grew like a dream pulled out of the dissipating crowd. She hesitated then, in the lobby, and the young man touched the small of her back again and the heat rose in her face. He inclined his head toward her, speaking in a whisper.

"Very important, miss. Please." What he had to tell her or show her seemed a burden to him, a weight across his skinny shoulders, and she thought at once that Houdini must have died from his escape, that he had suffered a brain hemorrhage or a poison in the blood. They arrived at the door of a room on the second floor.

When Anna stepped into the room, Houdini sat on a brocade couch, taking sips from a tiny cup. Next to him sat the Scotsman, trimming a cigar with his knife. Houdini wore a heavy white bathrobe belted tightly around him. He stood and smiled and bowed to her a little. His eyes were the color of pewter, his lips thick and feminine, his nose sharp and angular, like some instrument for cutting.

"Please, sit with us for a moment." His voice came high, laced with a slight accent; she noticed now how small he was, how muscular in his neck and face. The Scotsman did not look at her.

"Mr. Houdini, I thought . . ."

He held up his hand, brown with callouses. "You must call me Ehrich."

"You're not hurt?"

At this the Scotsman laughed out loud and lit his cigar with a match he struck against his boot sole. He threw the match into a green glass ashtray.

"No, I'm not hurt. But I do need your assistance."

The three men watched her. "How?" she said.

He explained that in the next hour he would arrive at the harbor, that the local constable would strip him, search him, and shackle him. He would be placed in a bag made of sailcloth drawn by chains. The bag would be nailed shut inside a shipping crate and the crate laced with anchor chains and heavy padlocks.

"Then," he said, "they lower me into the water." He smiled. "You won't see me for a while."

She shook her head. "I don't think it's clever, what you do. I think it's foolishness."

The Scotsman spoke up. "Last night, we saw a fine turning out at the Odeon Theatre. Watermen were there with a challenge escape." He puffed on his cigar. His words seemed directed at no one in particular.

"They bring out this sea monster, a giant octopus or a squid, I'm not sure. Bigger than a man, preserved in an ice box, a formaldehyde bath. They slit this monster open, push Houdini inside, sew the thing with piano wire. Two hours that escape. The preserving fumes nearly killed Houdini by the end."

He turned his cigar, studying the lengthening ash. "Before that," he said, "a zinc-lined piano box, an iron boiler, a milk can filled with water, an enormous leather football laced by experts." He looked at her. "Defying death, missy, is no foolishness."

She started to speak and Houdini took her hand.

"I can get out of the box, yes. But I'll need a key, for the manacles. Not even a key, really. A length of watch spring. A lockpick. Almost nothing."

She thought of what he would put himself through, the utter darkness, the cold, brackish water rising in the box.

"But the nails on the box, the chains. Why risk your life this way?"

He smiled at her, his lips tight and shiny as the skin on a fruit. "A tiny lockpick," he said. "Everything will be fine. No more than one of your hair pins."

She pushed away the hair that had fallen around her face. Houdini held his hands together, like a child at prayers.

"You'll help me?" he said.

"How would I help you?"

"You must give me the key. So no one sees it, after I have been searched."

"What's to keep anyone from seeing it?"

The Scotsman laughed, and the ash on his cigar broke off and fell across his vest. Houdini took her hand again.

"Before they lower me to the water, I'll be allowed a kiss from a pretty girl, for luck." He looked at her. "The key will be inside your mouth."

She yanked her hand away and stood, her face burning with the blood that pounded in her ears. She smoothed out the folds of her cape and her blue uniform, the patterns of the rugs beneath her feet blurring in her vision. She shook, hearing those words: *pretty girl.*

"I don't need to be here," she said. She turned to leave, and the Scotsman grabbed her above the elbow, squeezing her arm.

"For chrissakes, girl, we need one kiss from you. It's not as if we're asking you to—"

"Let her go." Houdini raised his voice and stood. The Scotsman chewed his cigar and walked across the room, his smoke drifting behind him.

"Let me explain further," Houdini said.

Anna looked at the part in his wiry hair, the creases around his mouth and neck. His carotid artery fluttered in a fold of skin, beneath a patch of whiskers he had missed shaving. Anna's eyes watered as heat spread across the back of her neck.

He reached out his hand. "Nothing more than this," he said. On his palm was an inch-long length of flattened clock spring, filed to a tear-drop shape. In her hand it felt cool, the metal shiny and bluish with tempering. She shook her head. Houdini reached as if to take her arms, then drew back. She saw him glance at the Scotsman.

"I have a reputation," Houdini said. "If you don't do this, if they find the lockpick on me, I'll be nailed in the box without the key. I *will* go in the water."

His gray eyes looked steady on her. They were eyes she'd seen before, eyes she knew as if from a dream. She started to speak, to hand back to him the length of spring. She remembered his eyes, the man touching his face as if to wipe away the rain, remembered imagining how they would look. They were these pewter eyes, Houdini's, as if he had stolen them to descend into the cold water and to see with them the blackness of the void, to bury their seeing forever in that box, to give them up to reputation, to the absence of a tiny key.

He showed her where to place the lockpick in her mouth, holding her chin and tipping her face toward the mirror. She let him, feeling him reach in like a dentist to touch her teeth and her gumline, the roof of her mouth. When the key was positioned, he told her to close her lips and smile. He examined her face.

"Relax the muscles here," he said, tapping her jaw. She thought of the doctors in the operating room, guiding her hands to clamp a cut blood vessel. When she had made herself relax, Houdini bent and pressed his mouth against hers, and his tongue lifted the key from her. His lips, cold and dry, tasted of metal.

"Everything just as I showed you," he said. "Don't change anything."

In the last hours of light Anna walked through the streets near the wharves, practicing again and again the placement of the lockpick in her mouth, believing she had forgotten everything he had shown her. From the top of Camden Street she watched as the crowds came out, drawing together on the wharves where market boats and paddle steamers sat docked, awaiting passengers and freight. Anna made her way through the crowds, the lockpick held tight in her mouth. Around the watermarks of the boats floated straw and rough boards and fish with their eyes whited and half eaten away by the gulls. The smell of the fish mixed with that of oil drifted shiny along the surface of the harbor. The gulls screamed and hovered on the wind.

The block and tackle had been rigged from one of the bollards at the end of the pier. The crate, thick and knotty, sat open, the hoisting cable and anchor chains curled on the dock planks behind it. A mule stood with its head hanging, the cable that would hoist the crate fastened to its saddle. Police erected barricades at the water's edge, so that no one would be pushed in by the force of the crowd.

Anna drew her cape around her, her hands bunched inside the folds of cloth. Twice the Scotsman came around and told her and the others standing near her to step back, not looking at her. The lockpick pressed into her cheek. It tasted of copper pennies, of sewing pins held in her mouth. She thought of her mother, watching for her through the curtains. She tried to think about the boy, tried remembering him, and saw his cracked lips, the rise of his ribcage, but not him, not his face. He might have had a tooth missing, but she couldn't remember.

The kiss would be short, as Houdini had shown her, so as not to raise any suspicion. He had told her she must not let the lockpick move, she must keep it secure inside her cheek. He would kiss her and that would be their only chance. It would not last and could not be repeated. He would enter the box. The water would take him. Wind lifted the edges of her hair and drew a chill down her spine. She dared not swallow. Her mouth filled with saliva like the beginnings of nausea. She clamped down on the wire with the muscles of her face and tasted her own blood.

A fringed carriage drew through the crowd, opening a

space in front of it that pulled in closed behind it. The carriage stopped and Houdini stepped out and waved to the crowd. A cheer went up and he nodded slowly without smiling. He wore a gray suit with a vest and a necktie, a stiff new collar.

A police sergeant stepped from the carriage behind Houdini, the brass buttons on his uniform tracing the curve of his stomach. He withdrew from the carriage a worn leather satchel, opened it, and lifted out with both hands a tangle of steel chains, handcuffs, leg irons, and padlocks. He shook them in the air, shouting to attest that he had inspected the manacles and found them to be unaltered in any way. The manacles clanked in his fist.

Anna touched her face where the lockpick lay hidden. The muscles of her cheeks and jaws quivered, and had numbed so that she could no longer feel the lockpick there. As she reached with her tongue to touch it, the pick slid atop her tongue. The taste of metal bloomed in her throat, gagging her. She nearly spat the wire out on the ground.

A committee of volunteers stepped forward to reinspect the shackles and to strip Houdini of his clothes. He removed his shoes and socks, his necktie and collar, his shirt and undervest. The men searched the spaces between his fingers, ran their hands through his hair, held matches near his ears and nostrils. They lifted his arms to search his armpits. One of the men put his fingers inside Houdini's mouth.

Anna used her tongue to push the wire back into the side of her cheek. For a moment she thought she had turned it, the point of it now directed at the back of her throat, but then she was unsure. She wanted to reach into her mouth to reposition it with her fingers, but of course she could not. Don't direct any attention to yourself, the Scotsman had told her.

The committee instructed Houdini to remove his trousers. Beneath them he wore only a tight breechcloth of thin white cotton. He stood hairless and pale, his muscles carving shadow in his skin. She saw through the thin fabric of the breechcloth his outline, distinct and full. She remembered the naked men in the emergency area after the paint factory explosion, remembered blushing as she moved among them, a girl of seventeen. She thought of the parents of the dead children, how they accepted their grief as if embarrassed by it, how they never touched. Throughout the crowd women turned away as Houdini stripped. The wire bit into the side of her mouth.

Several of the men held up a section of canvas as a screen, and a doctor was brought forth to complete the inspection. The men drew away the canvas and began to shackle Houdini. They locked his elbows with cuffs connected by a steel bar running across the middle of his back. Three sets of iron bands linked his wrists, joined by padlocks and chains to similar bands clamped around his ankles. Houdini raised his head as a heavy iron collar was hinged around his throat and padlocked at the back of his neck, the chains on the lock connected to those at his wrists. All of these were woven through with more chains, secured with padlocks.

They directed him to the crate, a man on either side of him. He walked with tiny steps, slightly bent like an old man, the chains dragging on the wood planks behind him. Anna shifted her weight and the wetness in her mouth ran to the back of her throat and she swallowed. For a minute she could not feel the wire and imagined she had swallowed it as well. Her mouth was numb. When she took a breath through her lips, the wire cooled at the back of her mouth. Houdini was lifted into the crate, the canvas bag pulled up to his neck and held there. The Scotsman poured brandy into a snifter and held it to Houdini's lips, shouting out words she only half heard. *The life of a man. The hand of God. The watery depths.* He had an actor's voice, loud and stagy. He would not look in her direction. She pushed the wire against the roof of her mouth to reposition it, and felt her heart beating in her temples, in her stomach. She wanted to let herself cry, to leave and forget all of this. The wire turned again and she pushed it forward, unable to remember where it had been when he had placed it in her mouth back at the hotel room.

"Some young lass," the Scotsman shouted. He extended his arms to the crowd. "One kiss, for fortune's smile." Her face burned and she stepped forward out of the crowd. The movement of the boats docked at the pier made her feel as if the world were in motion beneath her. Her legs quivered. Houdini stood with his gaze fixed out over the heads of the crowd. She knew that already he was at work, twisting his hands inside the canvas bag, positioning them. The Scotsman lightly held her fingers and brought her to the front of the crate as if leading her through a waltz.

The key was now only a coppery sourness in her mouth. Houdini looked at her, no flicker of recognition in his face. She leaned toward him, not knowing what to do with her hands. She wanted to touch him, to steady herself against him, to keep herself from falling. His face came up to hers and she smelled on him the sweetness of the brandy. Then his lips touched hers and she felt the sting of his whiskers, the dryness of her lips, the push of his jaw downward and her own pushed with it. His tongue ran between her lips, moving across her teeth. She parted her teeth slightly, then opened her mouth, and somewhere behind her the shouts of the crowd mixed with those of the Scotsman saying "maybe his last, maybe his last," and with her eyes closed her hands moved in the empty air, reaching toward him, and her fingertips brushed the canvas bag, the muscles of his face worked against hers and then his tongue slid fully into her mouth. A shuddering passed through her. Already too much time had passed, must have passed. They would know, she thought, and she angled her face slightly upward, tilting her throat, and inside her mouth she felt his tongue thicken and flatten, his saliva warmer than hers at the back of her throat. The key floated somewhere between them, the taste of it rising into her sinuses. She opened her eyes briefly and saw his gray eyes open and stilled in concentration. She closed her eyes again, and then the wind blew cool at the edges of her mouth, Houdini was shouting to the crowd that he would be allowed only twenty minutes, that the oxygen inside the crate would be depleted in three.

The Scotsman drew her back to the edge of the crowd. She watched Houdini wave to the crowd and smile at her, but it was a smile for the crowd; it told her nothing. The canvas bag was lifted up over him and his face disappeared from sight, his outline shifting and bobbing under the canvas. She imagined him in the bag, reaching with his fingers to withdraw the key, working already at the locks as the men chained shut the bag and folded it—him—into the crate. The box lid fell down and then the hammers sounded in the moist air, six of them pounding a strange, short song, like a children's song. The chains drew up the crate, the mule strained, and the box lifted and spun in the air. The men pushed it over the side of the pier and the crowd pressed forward to watch. It hit the water and bobbed, tilting slightly before it began to sink. The Scotsman withdrew his watch and began to count in quarter minutes, shouting, holding his watch up to the crowd. The crate fell fully out of sight in the black water, tiny waves splitting white around the cable. Anna leaned out to see, the press of thousands at her back. Still in her mouth were the sweetness of the brandy, the sourness of the key. She closed her eyes to imagine his frantic work in the blackness, in the failing air, the crate buried in cold, the warmth at its center, his warmth, his beating heart. The Scotsman sounded the minutes. She swallowed, tasting him. *Don't die,* she whispered.